aesthetic that rejected punk orthodoxy in favor of something much more magnificent and inclusive."

- Byron Coley, writer for WIRE Magazine,
author of C'EST LA GUERRE:
EARLY WRITINGS 1978-1983
and co-author (with Thurston Moore)
of NO WAVE: POST-PUNK.
UNDERGROUND.NEW YORK.. 1976-1980.

"A healthy authorial sense of curiosity and generosity lends weight to No Evil Star's intersecting lives, where Chris D. ably traces out the contours of human torment in a manner recalling American films of the 1970s."
- Grace Krilanovich, author of
THE ORANGE EATS CREEPS

**WHAT WRITERS HAD TO SAY ABOUT CHRIS D.'S ANTHOLOGY
A MINUTE TO PRAY, A SECOND TO DIE**

"Reading Chris D.'s blood-on-the-page prose is like running naked, screaming with terror and desire, through the fetid back alleys of American pulp culture. You're seduced, fucked over, doused with whiskey, set on fire, dragged by the getaway car, nailed by the hail from a 30.06 and still, still - you can't stop reading."
- Eddie Muller, author of
DARK CITY DAMES, THE ART OF NOIR and
the novels, THE DISTANCE and SHADOW BOXER

"...he continues a tradition in writing that is all but lost; authors who use their powers of imagination and creativity rather than simply recounting or inventing a memoir. Like the outsider artists that Chris D. champions, he writes for the future, for art, to someday be truly discovered for the great talent he is."
- John Doe, singer/songwriter
of X and The Knitters

"Chris D. presents...such an immense encapsulation of his life's work that it reads as literary autopsy of a man not yet dead but of one who has died a thousand times and somehow miraculously between crucifixions used pen as shovel to prevent himself from being buried alive."
- Lydia Lunch, musician and author of
PARADOXIA and WILL WORK FOR DRUGS

"To my mind, the lyrics he wrote...are as blinding a display of raw, universe-gobbling intelligence as have ever been penned...The sources from which Chris drew his inspiration are a classic pop cultural blend - exploitation films of all stripes, pulp fiction, French decadent poets, hot rod gangs, mystical Catholicism, underground biker comix, beatnik booze into the hippie acid continuum, and on and on and on. This is a mix that has gained great subterranean currency over the past few decades, but when Chris was churning through these waters, they were as yet uncharted. His written work (along with that of fellow travelers such as Exene Cervenka, Dave Alvin, John Doe and Claude 'Kickboy' Bessy) created a new, totally crazed hipster

SHALLOW WATER

A Poison Fang Book

Front and back cover designs by C. D.

ISBN: 978 0615869360

First published by New Texture, August 2012

First Poison Fang Books edition, October 2013

Printed in the United States

10 9 8 7 6 5 4 3 2 1

SHALLOW WATER

A SOUTHERN GOTHIC NOIR WESTERN

BY

CHRIS D.

POISON FANG BOOKS

FOR
JULIE CHRISTENSEN,
PETER ANDRUS,
WAYNE JAMES STEINERT (R.I.P.)
ROBYN JAMESON,
CAM KING,
REX ROBERTS
AND ALL THE OTHER FOLKS
WHO PASSED THROUGH THE RANKS OF
THE BAND DIVINE HORSEMEN...
WHEN WE WERE SINGING ABOUT
THESE NAIVE, SAD, ROMANTIC KINDS OF THINGS
AND
IN MEMORY
OF WRITERS
JAMES M. CAIN,
CORNELL WOOLRICH,
W. R. BURNETT
WHO ONCE
WROTE THIS KIND OF BOOK

1

The first time I saw her she was crawling along the edge of the muddy, empty street. She was trying to pull herself up on a hitching post when she spotted me.

"Please…help me up."

I could barely hear her, but I could tell she was pretty young. You wouldn't have known to look at her at first glance. I was surprised she could still open her mouth, let alone talk, because some courageous bastard had beaten the holy hell out of her. She was a wreck, yet beautiful and dark in a smoldering way that kind of made your head feel light. Black hair was matted down around her face and neck with mud, and her long lavender satin dress was torn. She brushed at it with bleeding fingers, revealing a fiery scarlet petticoat beneath. Stifling a sob, she tossed back her head.

"Please…I know you'll help me. You're not from around here."

Her voice was husky, thick with drink. Her eyes locked into mine as I reached down and pulled her up behind me onto the horse. She swayed, and I thought she was going to go all the way over the other side and land on her ass again. But she caught her balance and snaked her arms snug around my waist.

We headed up the street. It was after 4:00 AM on a Monday morning and, in a small town like that, you could lay five-to-one odds on seeing nary a soul stirring.

"I know it's late, mister, but we shouldn't be headed down this street right now. Not after what happened to me a little while ago."

It was the kind of thing I should have expected her to say. Whiskey was on her breath, but she hadn't gotten in her ravaged condition from just being drunk. She pointed to our right with a trembling finger.

"Take the alley there to the outskirts. We'll hit an orchard. That way we can get from town into the country without being seen."

"What makes you think I'm leaving town?"

She gave me a puzzled look.

"Town." I stared back. "I just got in, and I'm dead on my feet. I was looking forward to a good night's sleep on clean sheets."

She frowned, turning away from me, and mumbled, "You'd be disappointed. There aren't any clean sheets in this hellhole."

We were already nearly down the alley, and I could make out what looked like a grove of peach trees looming up ahead. A couple more minutes and the fragrant trees were all around.

"Now that you've talked to me, helped me, you'll want to get out of town. As far and as fast as you can ride."

I made a face. "I should have figured as much."

I reined in on the horse. "So what could happen to me just from making your acquaintance?"

Right then something small and silvery whistled by my ear. The horse bucked as the object thudded into the tree next to me. Even from six feet away in the dim moonlight and the shade of the branches, I could make out what it was. A bowie knife.

"You there! Stop dead in yer tracks!"

The cracked voice was slurred with drink. I'd had my Colt out as soon as the knife hit the tree, but I stayed relaxed.

She breathed heavily in my ear. "Don't stop for him. He's nobody. He can't hurt us."

"Hey, you! I said stop!"

I'd already stopped, but, from his blurry-eyed vantage point, I was undoubtedly still bearing down on him.

"I'm stopped."

"No, you ain't."

At the rate he was going, the horse's ass was going to wake up the whole damn town. He stumbled from the shadow of a peach tree about five yards away, a fat, wallowing blob of a man. He wheezed and coughed with each lurching step.

"Oh, it's you! What're you still doin' in town? The mayor told you to be across the county line by sunrise."

He waited impatiently, but she said nothing.

"Well, whore, you only got an hour to go!"

She still didn't answer and stared at me instead.

"And who the blazing hell're you?"

I smiled down at his flushed, perspiring head. A tiny, pinched face peered up questioningly from a doughy mass of mottled, pink flesh. He started to get worried when I didn't reply. Then he finally saw the gun.

"You a f-f-friend of hers, mister?" He stammered, "Sorry, if I startled you. I-I-I'm the caretaker here. Y'know, for the orchard, I mean. Gotta keep a watch on somethin' like this when it's this close to town."

I let the horse stray a few feet and plucked a ripe peach. The fat man's mouth went slack as I took a bite.

"Still didn't catch yer name, friend." He wasn't so drunk anymore. But he didn't have a gun. And it looked like he didn't have another knife, either.

I smiled faintly, "That's because I didn't give you one."

She smiled for the first time since I'd met her. I let the horse get a little closer to the tree, nodded at her, then at the knife. She casually reached over, like it was something she did all the time, and yanked the blade from the trunk. It made a whoosh sound as it came out. The fat man swallowed noisily.

"Now, honey, I was just joshing you a little. You know, funnin' you."

"You been funnin' me once too often, Gus. You and every other sneaking piece of man-trash in this town."

He didn't like that talk. If she'd been alone, he'd have been the brave son-of-a-bitch. But she wasn't, she was with me.

I realized I didn't know her name, so I introduced myself. "My name's Santo Brady."

She smiled through her stringy, ratted black hair. "I'm Lucy Damien."

"I'm Gus Howard."

We both turned to stare at him. He shot his eyes down to the ground, nervously shuffling his feet.

"I guess I'll be seein' you folks." He waddled backwards a few feet as if to leave. I cocked the gun, and he froze.

"Well, Gus, now that we're all acquainted, it seems a shame to break up the party. I'm just getting to know you."

"I gotta be gettin' back to the shack. My wife'll be bringin' me supper."

"He's lying. He ain't married."

I grunted pleasantly while he squirmed. "I'll tell you what, Gus. You come on over here, take the reins of my horse and lead us through the orchard into the hills out there on the other side. Then you can come on back and have your supper. How's that sound to you?"

He didn't answer right away. "You know, that's swamp there on the–the–other side. Gators are gonna be roamin' on out that way."

"I been in a swamp before, Gus. I was born in a swamp."

He went white. "You was?"

I nodded and caressed the barrel of my Colt. He swallowed again, slowly made his way over to us and grabbed hold of the reins. Without a word, he began leading us further into the peach grove.

I didn't ask her what she was supposed to have done that was getting her kicked out of town. I figured I'd find out soon enough. Gus knew, but he wasn't feeling too talkative anymore. He kept looking at us over his shoulder every few steps, nervous as hell.

"Say, you ain't the famous Santo Brady who spied for the Confederacy and got a reprieve from Abe Lincoln hisself for saving those pickaninnies from the burning orphanage, are you?"

I nodded when he glanced back at me, and I gave a wicked laugh. "Except ol' Honest Abe wasn't so honest on that one. It was a stunt for the newspapers. I was the one who started the fire." It was a lie, but I knew it'd give Gus something to think about.

Yeah, Gus was impressed, no doubt about that. But the girl couldn't have cared less. She'd lost interest, too tired and too beat to give a damn. Her head bobbed up and down with the horse, and her big brown eyes fluttered behind half-closed lids. A thin stream of blood trickled down her chin onto my shoulder. When I turned back to Gus, he was staring me straight in the eye. He had something up his sleeve.

"Whatsamatter, Gus?"

"Nothin'."

I let it go. I had other things that were bothering me, like my back and my behind. I was so sick and tired of being on that goddamn horse. I'd been riding pretty much seven hours straight and was more than ready to hit the sack. The girl had changed things. It would be a good couple of hours before I got any shut-eye.

That was when something funny started happening. If I hadn't been so tired, I probably would have noticed it a hell of a lot sooner. The horse was having trouble keeping its feet. I looked down, and it took me a few seconds to figure out exactly what was happening. We were sinking. The bastard had led us straight into quicksand, and I'd been too groggy to realize it. Even the mare had been too exhausted because she never would've strayed into muck like that when she was fresh.

Gus was standing slightly to the side, watching to see if I'd caught on yet. I hoisted the Colt level with his head and cocked the hammer.

"All right, you goddamn son-of-a-bitch! You still want to have a whole head when you wake up this morning, you take good hold of those reins and lead us right back out again."

"What?"

"What! This goddamn quicksand, that's what!"

He looked at me with stupid cow eyes, but his hands fumbled nervously. He'd led us out into a small patch right in the middle of the grove where there weren't any trees. A thin blanket of moss covered the bog.

"I ain't afraid of that gun, and I ain't afraid of that whore, and I ain't afraid of you!" He had his massive thumbs planted proud as punch behind his striped suspenders. I was beginning to lose my patience.

"I'll count to three, Gus."

"You shoot me, how'll you get out of that quicksand?"

"As the last thing I accomplish in this world, it'll give me some degree of satisfaction."

"It'd satisfy me, too." The girl had come back to life with new fire in her voice.

Suddenly, the horse whinnied, panicked, lurched forwards. She nearly pitched me over her head. Then the girl grabbed onto me to keep from falling, and the gun went off. Instead of shooting Gus' hat clean off like I'd intended, a small neat hole appeared in his forehead. His eyes rolled. With nary a sound, he fell face first down in the muck. He was stone cold dead.

"Good riddance."

I gave her a dirty look. "I wasn't going to kill him."

"Well, he's sure enough killed us."

I reached beneath her, grabbed the saddlebags and rifle, and heaved them to solid ground.

"You gonna lighten the load? Maybe make us so light we'll float right out of this stuff?"

I ignored her jibes. She laughed when I brought out the lariat.

"You're one of those cowboys you read about in dime novels."

I threw it, trying to lasso a branch on the nearest tree, but missed. The horse was really struggling now. Her legs had all but disappeared in the mud. That fat dead bastard. He was killing my horse as sure as if he'd still been alive. It kept making me madder and madder because there was nothing I could do to save her. I threw the lariat a third time, and it snagged the branch.

"Put your arms around my neck and don't let go no matter what!"

She did what I told her. I tugged at the rope to see if it would hold.

"Okay, I'm gonna ease off real slow."

We slid further into the stuff. We might as well have been taking a bath in cold grits, except this bathtub didn't have any bottom. And it kind of sucked at you like it was hungry for your bones. We started sinking fast, so I pulled along the rope, hand over hand, as hard as I could. The solid shore came a yard closer with the muck up around our shoulders. I heaved forwards.

"Try to stretch out your legs behind you and kick, like you were swimming."

She didn't say anything, just nodded. She grunted with the effort, and all at once, we gained another four or five feet. Something brushed against the toe of one boot. I figured the bottom was sloping up. We wrestled the rest of the way out and collapsed on top of Gus, both of us out of breath.

I almost fell asleep right there. Probably would have, too, if it hadn't been for that son-of-a-bitch getting cold under me and her firm, fleshy heat pressing into my back. She rolled off with a sigh of relief, and I struggled to my feet.

The mare whinnied. Her frantic eyes pleaded with me. Her head and neck were all that were above the surface, so I took up the Colt again and put a bullet in her brain. Her head stayed still like that for a minute, then slumped limply to the side, disappearing completely in the mud.

The girl had picked herself up and was staring at Gus' corpse. She spat on him as I yanked at his suspenders, sliding him the rest of the way into the quicksand.

2

We started walking. I wanted to get away from that town as fast and as quietly as possible. Gus could have friends. And, even though it was late, there was always the chance someone had heard the shots or would come out after him.

If I had any brains, I thought, I'd put a bullet in the girl's head, too, and lose some dead weight. I knew she was going to be trouble. It was written all over her. Even if she knew that country like the back of her hand, I kept thinking I should just turn her loose, both go our separate ways.

The moon was still high in the sky. It cast a blue light on her face that flickered with the shadows of the trees. She slightly tilted her head. Her eyes locked into mine, and I stopped walking.

She smiled, "Thanks for helping me. I'm sorry about Gus."

"How many more Guses are there?"

"Too many."

I made a face and turned away. From where the moon hung in the sky, I could tell we were heading west.

"There's a hollow about three miles southwest of here. It's a good hiding place if you want to get some sleep."

"You don't think it's too close to town?"

"Nobody from town'll go near there. Too many cottonmouths."

"And what about you and me? You think snakes give a good goddamn who they bite?"

"I know a spot where there aren't any snakes. The raccoons take care of them."

We walked another mile or so till we'd left the grove far behind. Another quarter of an hour went by, and we were well into the cane, not saying anything.

"So do you know the railroads around here?"

"Where do you want to go?"

"New Orleans."

She looked away.

"What's the matter?"

"I been there already."

"Yeah?"

"I'm not particularly crazy about going back."

"What makes you think you have to?"

"Nothing."

"That's right."

She faintly grimaced and whispered under her breath, "Yeah…"

"Listen, honey, you show me the railroad, point me in the right direction, and we'll part company."

She didn't say a thing for a few steps, then, "It's a good four miles. About three miles or so beyond that hollow."

We didn't talk much after that. She kept her eyes on the moon, following it like she was hypnotized, like some great pagan god held her in sway and was pulling strings with each and every one of her movements. Not quite like a puppet, because her body moved too smoothly, with too much grace and ease.

I looked down at her bare feet. Without taking her eyes off of the sky, she picked her way through the brambles and briars, circumnavigated stones, cane stumps, low hanging tree branches, like a blind person would.

Mist hung close to the muddy ground, a warm, wet vapor that cleaved to you, seeped through your clothes and made them stick to you. A second skin. It was the kind of mist you find in every swamp from the Everglades to the Bayou to East Texas. A living, blue-grey ghost of a thing that haunts your every step, in love with the heat and taut softness of human flesh.

Suddenly, it hit me that I'd been through that stretch of land before, maybe seven years previous, during the war. I don't know what made me realize it like that out of nowhere. Maybe it was the way the moon stared down, cold and sodden from the clear sky, the way the dead branches reached up for it. The moon was faintly reflected in the mud, but seven years before it had glared back at me from ankle-deep streams of blood.

I could see the whole picture in front of me again. Except back then there hadn't been so much underbrush and cane. That had been mashed flat by the horses and the foot soldiers. And then there'd been the heat. That next morning, the sun had been a round red ball of a furnace hanging low in the sky. I had been a little delirious all day, ever since I'd woken up. There'd been maybe an hour of sleep on the freight train. The remainder of our troop, the survivors, we'd hitched a ride in an empty cattle car all the way from Atlanta. As I'm sure you've heard, the bastard Sherman burnt most of the city to the ground. We'd been shocked to find a train still running, let alone a train without a bunch of blue belly sons-of-bitches hanging all over it. We'd fallen off in Coweta county because we'd known there'd be a blockade coming up pretty soon after that. It'd been swamp marsh and canebrake ever since.

We'd been wandering blind, hoping to find some trace of our division, something bigger than us that we could hook up with. Another thing we'd been looking for were horses, since we were cavalry. But the only ones we were running across were of the dead variety. Dead horses were the first sign that there'd been some fighting. It would've been funny if it hadn't been so horrible, but dead horses are what we always saw first when there'd been a battle.

Then came the men, if you could still call them that. Suddenly bodies would be everywhere. Bloody, muddy rag dolls. You couldn't tell blue from grey. Sometimes there'd just be pieces lying in pools of blood. You got used to it after a while. Seeing it three, four, maybe six or seven days a week for nearly four years, you couldn't do much else. Either that or go crazy. And there were plenty of fellows who couldn't figure the right take on it, couldn't keep it straight and not let it get under their skin. They got sent back pretty fast, because it didn't take them long to crack. And it didn't seem to matter how old they were, either. Boys barely into their teens or old codgers who should've been back at the general store smoking their pipes or playing checkers. It didn't matter. Once a man cracked, they never got completely back to normal. Not that I saw anyway.

I don't know how I did it. One thing I noticed, though, after I was discharged I'd developed a hell of a short temper. Just let any bartender take too long bringing me my beer or a fancy coat gambler look cross-eyed at me, and I'd be jumping down their throats. Sometimes it'd nearly get me killed. Or them killed. I'd had one sheriff in northeastern Texas crack me real good on the head from behind, then throw me in the pokey for a solid week. After that, he'd felt generous and kicked me out of town.

There'd been a little, black-haired Indian girl in Kentucky named Mildred who'd tried to calm me down. I wished that she had. One of the only regrets I have in my life is that I didn't let her. And she was the one who paid the price.

I'd gotten drunk on rye whiskey in a small log cabin saloon in Louisville, and she'd been trying to keep me out of trouble. It was perfectly jake with the owner because Mildred worked there. That was part of her job, keeping hotheads like me cooled down when we got to drinking too much. She was probably the best friend I'd ever had up to that point. I'd already known her for a good couple of months. We'd go fishing together every Sunday and have a picnic beside the lake in the early summer evenings.

But that day, the day it happened, I wasn't listening to her. I wasn't listening to anybody. It was everybody else be damned, and the devil take the hindmost. I'd gotten into an argument with some young buck in deerskin pants and a coonskin hat. I don't know who the hell he thought he was. He came in there wiping his feet on womankind in general, shooting his mouth off because he was stone drunk, too. Way worse than me. Way ruder and more foul-mouthed than I'd ever been.

The last straw was when he drew one of his nickel-plated revolvers from his fancy double holster and pretended to do something with it when Mildred walked by. Something lowdown and dirty. I'd told him he'd better wipe his wet nose and get-the-hell out before his mama came looking for him. Then he'd get in real trouble. A boy like that, it was the wrong thing to say. But his dirty mouth was the wrong thing for me to put up with after three beers and most of a quart of rye. Especially when it had something to do with Mildred. She let it roll off her back. Not me. Nobody talked about my girl that way.

She'd tried to calm the both of us down. When it didn't work, she'd looked over at Paddy, the bartender. But he didn't have the guts or the brains to fight his way out of a burlap sack. So, it had kept on getting worse. I don't even remember the son-of-a-bitch's name.

The way it ended up, Mildred got between us somehow just as we were drawing our guns. She got it from both sides. It was like somebody had thrown a red-hot poker down my throat. When the smoke cleared, she lay there dead, eyes wide open, two bullets through her chest and back.

The kid went bug-eyed at what he'd done. And, while he stood there puzzling out why my girl lay dead on the barroom floor, I blew his damn fool head off.

Just then, the sheriff had walked through the door.

That's how I'd gone to penitentiary. Prison. Behind bars for a long five years. I guess I was lucky. It could have been life. It could have been the gallows. But the bartender turned out to be good for something after all, testifying the way it had gone down. Not that it made much difference. Helping to shoot down my own girl, even by accident, was ten times worse than anything the judge could have handed out. Worse than anything that had happened to me during the war.

"What're you thinking about?"

I looked at her, suddenly broken out of my reverie. So I told her the whole story, and when I was finished I asked her about her past.

"I don't know you well enough yet. If we're together long enough, I'll end up telling you."

It had to be at least five in the morning. The sun would be rising anytime.

"Here it is, the hollow I told you about."

"I don't see any cottonmouths."

"I guess they smelled you coming."

Her idea of a joke. I smiled faintly. "Maybe so."

I paced the clearing there and turned back to her. "Let's get some shut-eye. It looks like this is the driest ground we'll see for some little bit."

We removed some underbrush, tidying up a spot for us to sleep, but there was a sudden movement at the base of a large oak tree. A long, elastic shape slithered in the darkness. I saw its eyes and the moonlight gleam on its fangs as it sprang out at me. I drew my Colt and split the cottonmouth's skull with a single bullet.

"Good shot." She smiled warmly after she said it. I gave her a good look up and down and realized she hadn't been scared at all. That kind of got to me, because it sure as hell had scared the piss out of me.

Then I heard something else, something I'd heard once before during the war when I'd been in Mississippi – a kind of nervous rustling.

"Damn!"

Now she looked scared. "What was that?"

"I'm not sure. But if it's what I think it is, we might just be sleeping in this here oak tree."

Sure enough, I started hearing a series of low, guttural snorting sounds.

"Okay, honey, upsy-daisy." Dropping the saddlebags and the rifle, I cupped my hands into a stirrup. She didn't need much more encouragement than that. She grabbed hold of the bottom branch as the first razorback broke into the hollow. I roughly shoved her skywards, clutched at the same branch and swung up into the tree.

All at once, a whole herd of angry, spooked wild boars came plowing through the small clearing. They saw us and congregated around the trunk, grunting, squealing and snorting as they stamped their hooves into the ground.

We sat up there in that goddamn tree looking down at them, at first laughing, then looking at each other, the back down at them like we were taking turns. And then not laughing anymore.

Her good looks kept drawing my eyes back to her. I don't know what it was. She wasn't God's gift to creation or anything. But there was this something. Something I'd once seen in a freed slave girl in Atlanta that gave me goose bumps, made my blood run cold. I hadn't really looked at a woman like that in quite a while. I hadn't been letting myself. I thought it'd keep me out of trouble if I just kept my feelings – and my hands – to myself. But she was the kind of woman who brought things out of you no matter how hard you tried to keep things hidden. And she seemed like she probably enjoyed and hated it both, what she could do to a man.

Right then I caught myself looking at her that way, that way I didn't want to. She seemed so strong and independent one minute, then willowy, yielding, vulnerable the next. She glanced away from me. She could feel it, too, and didn't want to start anything – at least not up in some goddamn tree.

"They're gone."

I stared dumbly at her, then realized the razorbacks had shuffled away from the trunk and back into the brush. The saddlebags and rifle were a mess, trampled to bits and covered with pig shit. I was lucky I had my money in my trouser pockets.

"I guess we should wait a few minutes."

I didn't answer her. I studied the branches up above us and found what I wanted. Luckily, the tree was huge. There was a bough about ten feet long and three feet thick ascending in a gentle slope.

I stood to get a closer look. It was horizontal and just flat enough to sleep on.

I could feel her eyes following my every move. "Don't tell me you're thinking what I think you're thinking!"

"Sure, it'll be okay. There aren't any wildcats in these parts. And there aren't any alligators or razorbacks that can climb trees, at least that I know of."

She looked at me, doubtful, then nervously smiled.

I climbed up to the broader branch, swept away the dead leaves, then reached down to her. She wasn't looking at me then. She was staring at the ground.

"What's the matter?"

She didn't answer right away. Slowly, she raised her face and stared at the moon. "Nothing's the matter."

I smiled, "Aren't bashful, are you?"

She slapped my hand petulantly, made a face, then climbed up beside me on her own. A piece of her satin dress caught in a jagged outcropping. She tugged at it impatiently, ripping the scrap off and revealing the black and scarlet mesh silk petticoat. I gave her my hand to steady her, and she reluctantly took it. That was when I noticed the wedding ring. A simple gold band on the third finger of her left hand. She caught me gawking and yanked her hand free.

"It's not what you think."

"What do I think?"

"That I'm married, I got a husband."

"Well, don't you?"

"In a way..." She looked back up at the sky. "But it's not what you think."

I got comfortably horizontal while I waited for her to explain. She said nothing more and lay down on the bough next to me, her left arm stretched back languidly behind her head.

I shrugged.

"I'll tell you. But not tonight."

With that she turned over on her side, facing away and giving me a scant few more inches of space. I rolled over, too, with my back to her, looking the way we'd come, trying to spot if there was anyone on our trail. There wasn't a soul stirring that I could see. No lights, no sounds, except the noises of the marsh and the canebrake.

I couldn't get to sleep. I tried to relax, but things kept coming back to me, things I hadn't thought about in a long time. I don't know what it was that started me brooding. Maybe it was her. It was something I'd done my damnedest to stop – dwelling on things in the past you couldn't change. All it did was make me more unhappy than I was already. I'd done enough of it in penitentiary.

I wanted to get to New Orleans, then on to Texas or even Indian Territory – somewhere where there wasn't so much law breathing down your neck.

3

I guess I must have dropped off for awhile, because when I opened my eyes again, the sun was poking its head over the hills to the east. Then I noticed something odd, a smell like something was cooking. I whirled around to find her gone.

"Hey, cowboy."

I stared down at the foot of the tree. There she was, crouched on her haunches in front of a small campfire, roasting something on a makeshift spit. I grabbed my hat and slid down the trunk to stand beside her.

"What're you doing?"

"What does it look like? Fixin' your goddamn breakfast."

I circled her, not quite believing my eyes. "What is it?"

"Possum. I borrowed Gus' knife." She picked it up off the ground, then wiped the bloody blade on her dress. "Sorry, I got it dirty." She handed it up to me, and I took it, tucking it back into my gun belt.

"It's the funniest thing. Whenever I cook possum, it tastes like fried chicken. Whenever anybody else cooks it, it tastes just like possum."

She took a stick, skewered part of the meat away, then held it out. "We don't have anything to drink."

I took it from her.

She tore hungrily at her piece.

"When was the last time you ate?"

She wiped her mouth with the back of her hand. "Day before yesterday. Rice, biscuits and collard greens."

Well, it was good, and it did taste like chicken, although how she managed that without all the spices and other things found in a kitchen, I'll never know. It wasn't the last time she'd surprise me.

After we finished wolfing down our breakfast, we started up walking again.

"There should be a stream of fresh water somewhere along here before we hit the railroad. You thirsty?"

I nodded. The sun was high up in the sky by then and hot as hell. The air was Indian summer thick with a sticky wetness. I scratched at the mosquito bites on my face and neck that I'd gotten during the night.

"You should've used this. I forgot to give you some before you fell asleep." She had a tiny, oval wooden case in her hand full of a yellow paste. "It's a salve I made from a plant down here. The bugs hate it."

I reached out, held the stuff up to my nose and winced. "I can see why. It stinks." I smiled and handed it back to her. I figured that we must have been getting close to the Alabama state line.

"We'll be hitting the state line soon."

She said it all sure of herself, then looked at me like she knew what I was thinking, like she could read my mind.

"Where you from?" I asked.

She didn't answer. It seemed like anything in her past was a real sore subject with her.

"Well?"

"You sure do ask a lot of questions, cowboy."

"I ain't a cowboy. Never worked with any cattle and never will. I hate the smell of 'em."

She laughed. "You must be a gunfighter then."

"I guess that strikes you as a pretty funny idea."

She nodded, smirking, trying to suppress her laughter.

"I worked as a bounty hunter for a short while after the war, before I went into the penitentiary. I wasn't fond of killing, unless it was necessary. I usually brought them back alive, unless they didn't give me a choice."

"Did you ever hear of me? Lucy Damien, sheriff killer?"

I stopped, puzzled, thinking she was pulling my leg. "No, I

haven't been keeping up on who's wanted by whom for whatever since I got out. Where were you supposed to have killed this sheriff?"

"A tiny hole-in-the-wall outside Little Rock called Sweet Home." She laughed. "This sheriff came after me with a branding iron after a bunch of cowboy sons-of-bitches had been banging away at me all night."

I stared at her, not sure what to believe.

"I'd been lazy, not keeping up my guard. It was about a quarter mile outside of town on this tiny farm. The fella I was with kept feeding me drinks, and I'd just gotten a letter from home, so I was in the mood. Then he brought his pals in from outside. I scratched and bit and howled, but they were too much for me. They held me down on that floor till way after the sun came up. Finally, when the bastards had to take a rest, I grabbed one of their pistols and plugged two of 'em in the head before they knew what hit 'em."

She stared into space for a few seconds, remembering painful things.

"Paulie, my beau," she said with venomous sarcasm, "He ran out to town to get the sheriff. I just lay there, I was so beat. Every muscle in my body ached. I was bleeding from between my legs. Before I knew it, the sheriff, Willie Tatum, busted through the open door. My valiant protector, Paulie, peeked over Willie's shoulder, scared to death at what I was going to do next. Willie sauntered over to the cowboys I'd killed, all manly, real cock-of-the-walk, and laughed. He stared back at Paulie, full of contempt for the spineless jellyfish who could let his gal go that far, let her get hold of a six-shooter and drill his partners full of lead. So, Willie says, 'Lil' girl, I'm gonna teach you a lesson you'll never forget for as long as you live.' He kicked the Colt lying by my side into the corner, then yanked me up so hard I thought my arm was going to come out of the socket. I'd been in a daze until then, but that snapped me out of it. I screamed, and he roared with laughter. He smacked the cabin door aside, and the sun hit me full in the face so I was blinded for a minute. 'Paulie, yer gal here needs a severe lesson in female docility.' Paulie looked at him funny because he didn't know what that word meant. I was hurting too much to appreciate Willie's mastery of the English language. Anyway, he dragged me through the dirt and tied both my wrists to the lowest rung of the corral gate while I tried to kick him between the legs. He thought that was funny. He told Paulie to go stoke up the fire in the cabin's fireplace. Paulie kind of looked at him stupid like he didn't know what Willie was up to, and Willie yelled at him to get-the-hell in there and do as he was told. That he'd see a wilder show than any I'd ever put on in any dance hall."

She paused, raised her head and shaded her eyes as she squinted up at the blazing sun. "Damn, I'm thirsty." She licked her lips, then remembered where she was in the story.

"Well, I don't have to tell you, I was getting plenty scared when he started in about building up the fire. I couldn't figure out what he was going to do until he pulled the branding iron out from behind the water trough. It belonged to his farmer brother – who just happened to own the cabin – and it was his brand, a big T with a cross in the middle. Willie stood there licking his chops like he'd done a thousand times before in the dance hall where I worked in Sweet Home. Finally, Paulie poked his head out of the cabin and said the fire was going pretty good. Willie took one last look at me, laughed, then ran to the door. I knew I had to get that rope free from my hands, or I was going to have one hell of a sore butt. I twisted and turned and pulled every which way, but I couldn't do it. He had that damn hemp too tight. It was scraping the flesh off my wrists. Then he was back there standing over me. The branding iron was glowing, red hot. He yanked and tore my petticoat away so my thighs were exposed. I kicked and screamed, but Paulie held me while Willie did it real quick. I passed out, it hurt so bad. Then suddenly, I was awake again, groggy as hell, them pouring whiskey down my face and falling all over themselves, laughing. I could barely see because it stung like crazy."

I stared at her, not quite believing the whole story.

"Paulie untied me, and Willie starts in with, 'Hey, you lil' bitch, it's better than gettin' yerself hung, ain't it?' He took a pull on the whiskey bottle, and I reached up and grabbed Paulie's gun from his holster. I shot Willie in the head. Then I got up, spat in Paulie's quaking face and plugged him, too. I thought it was a good time to get out of Arkansas after that."

She frowned at my doubtful look, then hoisted her dress up above her stockings and garters. And there it was, emblazoned in a livid purple welt of scar tissue, the T with a cross in it.

"I'm lucky it didn't gangrene up on me. I wouldn't be here telling you the tale if it had."

"You still didn't answer me, honey."

"What?"

"Where are you from? Where do you call home?"

She shook her head in disbelief that I didn't seem more impressed.

"I was born and raised in St. Louis." She changed the subject again. "You know what they call Arkansas?"

I wagged my head to say no.

"The Land of Opportunity!" The woods rang with her laughter. "The only opportunity I ever got there was to die." She stopped laughing. "Well...I guess we better head on."

We started walking again. She was a funny gal with what seemed like more guts than most men I'd known. The better I got to know her, the more it struck me we had in common.

Then something else struck me. Just as she made me think about things I hadn't thought about in a long time, she made me forget things, too. Things that had been burned into my brain as sure as that brand had been burned into her hip.

"Now what's the matter with you?"

I looked up from the mud we were in and saw her standing petulantly a few yards ahead. I hadn't realized that I'd stopped dead in my tracks.

"Nothing." I started again and caught up with her.

"You're lying."

I didn't want to talk about it. She'd made me forget what I'd come home to after the war. She'd made me forget for just a few minutes. Somehow, that made it worse.

"What is it?"

"You don't want to know."

"Why?" she asked indignantly, "Is it that horrible?"

I nodded. "That's what I can't figure. What you've got inside you that made me forget it like that. It's the kind of thing you can't forget, not ever. It's something that you carry around inside you, just like that brand."

She gave me a funny look, and we kept on walking.

"Okay. Don't tell me."

"You swept it out of my head for a few minutes. It was a real shock when it hit me again."

We covered another few yards in silence, picking our way through brambles and briars.

"I was a wreck after the war – like everybody else. I came home with my sanity barely intact. But my home wasn't there. My folks had had a small farm in Tennessee. We weren't rich or anything like some of the other landowners in the county. But we were doing okay. Pa was away a lot up North trying to set up deals for the tobacco and cotton we grew. I didn't have any brothers or sisters, so Ma and me ran things. We worked really hard right alongside the slaves."

"That's what every Johnny Reb with a guilty conscience says nowadays."

The words stung, and it was all I could do to keep from slapping her.

"This'll sound funny to you, but they were more like part of the family. Not that they slept in the main house with us or anything, but… they ate with us and were treated right. I don't pretend that owning somebody's okay. We didn't look at them like they were animals like a lot of whites did."

She interrupted. "You don't have to apologize for being a son-of-a-bitch. Let those bastards who've never done any wrong start throwing stones. You don't know the wrong I've seen, that I've walked through – and some of it that I've done – and come through the other side, my head held high. The world is a miserable place. My mother was Blackfoot Indian. My father didn't care. He was a very religious man, a man with principles that had some sense. At least, back then. He was also the only kind man I've ever met. Kind as hell. Except to me." She spit the words out, hurt, bitter, unyielding.

I could see the Indian in her, and it made me feel good. I don't know why, when you think about where I'd been raised.

"So, what is this thing that I made you forget?"

I took a deep breath. "I hadn't even come within fifty miles of the farm since '63. Pa's heart had given out, and he died later that year. I'd tried to get home to see Ma, but it was impossible. I thought about deserting. I thought all the stuff any soldier ever thinks about when they're killing men day-in, day-out. Why? What for? And when you start asking yourself that question, it's time to put down your gun. The things about the Confederacy I admired, what had held sway with me up till then in the darkest hours of the war, through all the mercenary, self-serving monsters I had run into, whether they were captains or majors or colonels or even generals, made me stay. Things I knew about General Lee from when I was in camp with him and saw him and heard him talk. Even monsters like Quantrill and Anderson up Kansas and Missouri way. There was something in there, inside of the blackest heart of the Confederacy – and there were as many black hearts and blackguards wearing grey as wearing blue – that something held me. But it slowly turned to ashes in my mouth.

"I came home in '65 and found something a hundred times worse than nothing. I found Ma. She was lying in the very middle of the burnt timbers."

I cleared my throat, because I didn't want to start bawling all of a sudden. She looked at me with sad eyes – eyes that knew what it was like to lose everything and still keep on going.

"She was just a pile of blackened bones. I wasn't sure at first. Then I saw the ring, the wedding ring on her left hand. Something that those ghouls of Sherman's command hadn't grabbed. It was amazing it hadn't melted in the fire. And it was her. Because there, inside the rim, was the inscription that Pa had engraved there. Hell, the way they loved each other, it was Death and whatever lies beyond, and you'd never ever, ever see those two lovebirds part."

I stopped because I couldn't go on.

She stared down into the mud as we walked and said nothing.

"She'd let the slaves go, the five or six we had. She'd set them free at the start of the war. It was more her doing than Pa's. Pa hadn't wanted to, but he'd let her have her way. She'd had this feeling that if they stayed, they wouldn't have had a chance. They all left, except for Eugenie, the cook, and her old husband, Pete. They wouldn't leave. And I found their bones, too, in those goddamn ashes. I laid down in those ashes and cried all day long. I'd never felt worse in my whole life. My best friends having their asses mangled and their heads split in two. There I was staring face-to-face with hell, a nothingness that made my quick, drunken temper ten times worse, so that by the time I hooked up with Mildred in Louisville…Christ, she didn't have a chance."

We both stopped because we'd come to a stretch of cleared land, maybe ten or fifteen acres. You could just spy the railroad line slightly elevated in the trees beyond. A rickety covered wagon stood by itself in the middle of the field.

"Maybe they've got something to drink, something besides spring water." She was right. A pull on a jug of something strong, something with a good kick to it, would sure as blazes make the both of us feel better.

There was something funny about that wagon, though. They weren't homesteaders on their way west. The color and patterns of the canvas cover was closer to a medicine show.

When we got nearer, I spotted the bearded man. He was wrapped in a suit of worn black clothes and had a preacher's hat covering his long, greasy hair.

"Looks like he's doing some kind of dance." She made a face after she said it, as if to say, "Here we go running into some crazy wild man out in the middle of nowhere."

Sure enough, he was waving something frantically in the air, something long and elastic.

"My God!" she exclaimed, "He's dancing with a goddamn snake!"

The closer we got, the less I liked it. But what was there to like about a lunatic preacher man cavorting with his pet snake?

"Yer poison ain't half as virulent as Man! Ye know that! Ye can sink yer fangs into me, my brother, act as the only true testament of our Lord Jesus Christ! That's what ye be! My tool destroying the venom of heathen loins!"

Lucy laughed at that last bit, and he jumped around like somebody had jerked a string. He narrowed his eyes. "Who be ye?"

"We're on our way to the railroad. We want to catch a freight to Louisiana."

He eyed me suspiciously, then gaped at Lucy. "Ye be dressed like a harlot out of Sodom! Have ye no shame!"

Lucy stopped smiling. "Sorry, mister. It's all that I had clean to wear this morning."

He didn't pick up on her sarcasm.

She put her hands on her hips and cocked her head to one side. "Excuse this interruption of your high mass here out amidst the cowpies, but we thought you might have something to drink. For the right price."

His eyes brightened up. He carelessly slung the cottonmouth around his neck and rubbed his filthy, bony hands together.

"I might be able to assist ye, Ma'am. There be a jug hangin' on the back of my wagon."

We both started to move in that direction, giving him and his snake friend a wide berth, when he blocked our way. "Ye pay the piper first. Tithing for our Lord's mission."

Lucy reached into her low-cut bodice, holding her large breasts steady with her other hand.

I moved forward, keeping one eye glued to him in case he tried anything funny with the snake.

Lucy came out with a single silver piece and tossed it to him. He struck out at it, catching like he was a snake himself.

I came up to the back of the wagon, still looking at them, when I heard a noise. I jumped, startled, and peered into the shadowy insides. There was somebody in there, a woman humming a low, strange melody to herself, rocking back and forth in a dilapidated rocking chair. She bent forwards into the light, and I had to suppress an involuntary gasp. I could hardly believe my eyes. She was a black girl of about

eighteen years of age with long, straight black hair, very pretty –
except for the fact that she had no eyes. No sockets, not anything there
but smooth, shiny skin on both sides of the bridge of her nose. She, too,
had a cottonmouth draped around her neck. She stroked the snake's
head as she reached out with her other hand, picked up a cracked jug
and handed it to me.

"You lookin' for this, I reckon."

I didn't say anything for a few seconds, then reached up and
took it. Hoisting it to my lips, I took a long pull and nearly choked. The
preacher man laughed.

"You okay?" asked the girl in the wagon.

I managed a "Yeah," cleared my throat, then took another pull.
It went down a little easier that time. I tossed it to Lucy. She took a
gulp, but immediately spit it out.

The preacher cackled with laughter.

Lucy wiped her mouth with the back of her hand. "This stuff
might as well be kerosene!"

"'T'aint but corn whiskey, Ma'am, with a lil' gunpowder
throwed in for medicinal purposes."

The black girl stepped down from the wagon, reaching her
hand out for me to help her. She knew I was hesitating because of the
snake.

"Don't you worry, Mister. He won't bite you. He ain't never
hurt nobody."

I helped her down, keeping an eye on the snake.

I couldn't figure how these two were getting away with all that
crazy cottonmouth handling. I'd known a few carnival people in my
time, but they had ways of keeping a snake's venom out of their veins.
Usually they would've sewn the snake's jaws shut with silk thread the
color of the snakeskin. But there weren't any such shenanigans being
pulled by these two.

"That be my wife, Camille."

Lucy was clearly in shock at the sight of the eyeless woman.

"You. sister, have a calling from God, from our dear Lord,
Jesus Christ, an' you are denying Him."

Lucy's expression changed suddenly. She stepped towards
Camille, and Camille reached out her hand, "Ain't I right, sister?"

"The name's Lucy." Her whole demeanor had changed. She
said it sober as hell.

"I knew it. Amen, Lucy!" Camille laughed, and her husband
looked troubled. Lucy took hold of Camille's hand and let the blind girl

lead her to the far side of the wagon, then to a large oak stump beside the line of trees skirting the railroad.

I shook my head, wondering if what had been in that jug was making me see things. Or maybe it was some rare vintage of instant salvation that had hit Lucy over the head like a sledgehammer, but left me immune. The preacher was as baffled as me. He snatched off his hat, scratched his head as he watched them whispering to each other, then walked to the wagon and roughly tossed the hissing cottonmouth out of sight.

"What name ye go by?"

"Santo Brady."

"Mortimer Elijah Hickock, first cousin to James Butler Hickock, the exalted sinner of Abilene most folks call Wild Bill."

I'd heard of Hickock before, knew a few crazy fellows who'd been stupid enough to tangle with him when they were on a weeklong drunk in Texas. But this Mortimer being Hickock's cousin struck me as either bald-faced lie or tall tale. Then I remembered something one of those fellows had told me, the one who'd survived the meeting with Wild Bill. He'd been lucky, getting only a nasty hole in his right cheek and a couple of teeth shot to smithereens. His breath had rattled and whistled when he named his and Wild Bill's mutual home town.

"Ye don't believe me? No matter."

I asked him where Hickock was born.

"All the poison-filled pages of those dime novels say he was born in Chicago. It ain't true. He come into this world and be baptized with his Christian name, James Butler, in Troy Grove."

Mortimer seemed to be telling the truth.

"So, ye be headed to Louisiana?"

I nodded. "And on to East Texas eventually."

He looked as though I'd struck him with lightning. "Ye mention the one abysmal geography where hell erupts onto the earth. Texas be a nefarious kingdom of killers, harlots and heathens. A demon desert ruled by government-bred nigger police. Yea, yea, a nigger police force makin' outlaw murderers seem saintly by comparison. Black, blue-gummed bastards who used to be slaves, freed after the war and turned loose, not only on plundering evildoers and hostile Injuns, but on proud refugees of the gallant Confederacy who fled into that no man's land with dignity barely intact. Refugees seeking asylum and to hold their heads up high, only to find the most brutal form of racial retribution."

He was in full swing then, sermonizing with a vengeance and ignoring the seeming contradiction shown by the skin color of his very own spouse.

"Blue-gummed, black banshees, like the ones be found in Georgia. The kind that can kill ye with their gangrenous bite."

He went on like that for a while longer, but I had stopped paying attention to him. I snuck off a glance at Lucy listening to Camille's wild declarations with something akin to rapture. What was going on there in that pasture was starting to get to me. And, hell, I thought, I didn't even really know this Lucy Damien. Whatever Camille was coming out with was putting Lucy through the wringer. Camille would raise her hands up to heaven, point north, then gesture wildly in a sweeping, all-encompassing arc. Lucy wiped tears from her cheeks with the backs of her hands.

I started over to them, but the preacher man stopped me.

"Tread lightly, son."

I looked down around my feet to find three cottonmouths and a diamondback swarming about my ankles.

"Mr. Hickock, you don't call home your bird dogs, I'm going to drill everyone one of them between their goddamn beady eyes!"

"Ye ain't got nothin' to fear, son. They be as gentle as kittens as long as I'm around."

I stepped outside the ring of snakes, and they ignored me. Maybe the old con was telling the truth. Suddenly, I felt my right pantleg snag and something smooth and sharp ventilated boot leather. One of the cottonmouths had bitten into my boot and was clinging with an iron-vise grip by one fang. I drew my Colt, fanned the hammer and exploded the heads of all four snakes. Mortimer screamed in horror at my depletion of his menagerie.

Lucy and Camille paid us no mind. They didn't even turn their heads when Mortimer went for the pitchfork lashed to the side of the wagon. I shot it out of his hands, and he dropped to his knees with an agonized shout.

"Damn ye! Damn ye!"

Camille laughed. "That man don't know his master, Mr. Santo. But yer wife showed me the true power you hold."

My wife! "She ain't my wife!"

"Mr. Santo, in spirit and under the eyes of Jesus, she shall be. She shall certainly be."

While I puzzled over her crazy talk, Mortimer fell face flat to the ground, holding his bleeding right palm and groaning with pain and humiliation.

"C'mon, Lucy. Let's get the hell out of here."

Lucy slowly rose to a standing position. She kissed Camille on the lips. Camille smiled, all the while stroking the head of the docile cottonmouth hanging around her neck.

4

We'd left Mortimer and Camille behind a long time past, at least two hours. Still, no freight had chugged down the line we followed.

Dry, red eucalyptus leaves littered the rail ties, burnt brittle by the sun. Weepy cypresses drooped before us so you could barely glimpse the railroad more than ten yards ahead at a time.

"What did she mean by that 'wife' business?"

Lucy didn't answer right away, staring at the rails, kicking the leaves with her blistered barefeet.

"She told me about my ties."

"Your ties?"

"My ties here on earth and my ties outside this life."

I pointed at her ring finger. "And what about your real husband?"

She didn't reply. I'd expected as much.

Then there was a noise behind us, the sound of a locomotive. I pulled her off the track into the shelter of a cypress. She yanked away from me but stayed under the tree.

It was still a few minutes before the locomotive pushed aside the overhanging branches and sputtered and coughed into view.

"Good. It's coming nice and slow. We shouldn't have any trouble at all."

I figured it wasn't going to be a very long train, so I waited until only the ninth or tenth carriage. The locomotive had already wheezed around the bend ahead of us, so there wasn't much danger of being spotted. I tagged an open, empty cattle car.

"Wait till I get in, then I'll pull you up."

She looked at me uncertainly as we trotted along beside the cars. "Don't worry. It's a cinch."

I got a smile out of her as I hopped aboard. She broke into a run, I nodded, and she leapt up into my arms. I caught her and fell backwards with her full on top of me.

"It looks like we're headed for Louisiana, honey."

She must've liked the way I called her honey because she gave me a kiss. And it didn't take much on my part to give her a good kiss back. We lay like that for a while, not saying anything. She felt good pressed against me, her bony hips digging into my thighs and her fleshy breasts flattened against my chest. She nestled close to my ear, her breath hot and quick, After a few minutes, I eased the both of us further back into the car. She didn't resist.

It had been months since I had been with a gal all close and feverish like that – unthinking, just following a pre-ordained set of reflexes that only the two of us knew. She slipped out of her dress so easy. And there she was, pale and slender with her heavy breasts standing out from her bony ribcage.

Before I knew it, my clothes were strewn in the hay, too, and the smell of the steers left over from the last time the car was cleaned went out of my head. Her thick, pliant lips mashed into mine.

That unthinking, reflexive feel suddenly went, and it was something I'd never known before. There she was, a reflection of something deep inside me that I couldn't put a finger on. One minute I saw things that made me want to beat the daylights out of her, the next minute I wanted to take care of her and protect her and shower her with riches for the rest of her life. I'd only known her a day, and already I would've stood up and died for her.

The air was hot and still, even though the car was moving. And, if a breeze did suddenly snake its way through the rickety, wooden slats, it was oppressive, smothering. When we finally fell away from each other, we were drenched with sweat. I fought to breathe for a minute and turned over on my stomach, propping myself up on my elbows. She laughed, reached over and rubbed the heel of her hand into the back of my neck.

"How long've you had that?"

"What?"

"That thing in your lungs."

"The asthma? Since I was a baby."

She sat straight up and stared at me with concern.

"It's okay, it'll pass. It always does."

"And I bet when you drink a lot, it makes it worse."

"Sometimes." I sat up. "How do you know so much about it?"

"My mother had it pretty bad. It always got worse when she drank. Especially if it was wine."

"Is that how she died?"

She just looked right through me, stoic, impassive, then slowly turned her head away. I pulled my trousers back on and crawled to the open door. I was getting used to her not answering half of my questions. I suppose that was one of the things that had me so hooked on her, that goddamn mystery.

I turned. "How far you headed?"

She shook her head and shrugged.

"What's wrong with New Orleans? Did you get into some kind of trouble there? Like back in that little town we just came from? Or like you did up in Arkansas?"

"Maybe."

"Kill somebody?"

"Maybe. Maybe not."

I gazed out at the passing marsh and cane.

"You ever heard the word 'pimp'?"

I nodded. "Of course." I knew what was coming then and didn't like it. Not one bit.

"After I left my husband, I went to Arkansas. Little Rock. After that trouble, I drifted south to New Orleans. I only wanted to get an honest job and make some money. I started off waiting tables at a steakhouse in the French Quarter. Then I met a man. He could tell I used to dance in dance halls, and he offered me a job. I was kind of afraid of him. Not because he was mulatto, or anything like that – that didn't mean a damn to me. I guess it must've been his eyes. One stared off-kilter, rolled off to the side when he'd had some drink. But he was real nice at first. I said okay, that I'd give it a try, and he gave me an address, told me when to show up. The first couple of weeks, I was just in the chorus line at the place. And, like he said, the money wasn't too bad…"

She pulled her dress over her head and smoothed it down.

"So, I let my guard down again and kept it up. It's funny, but I was actually having a lot of fun. Then one night, Dan, my boss with the lazy eye, brought this big, fat redneck bastard backstage. He was some kind of politician, was big friends with the mayor, owned a lot of land and had tons of money to throw around."

I knew what was coming, and it surprised me that I gave a damn. I almost stopped her right then and there, but I'd been asking for it, to know about her past. Besides, if I didn't hear her out, it'd probably start eating away at my insides.

She nodded. "Yeah, he wanted me to take the old goat home. I said no and slapped Dan's face right in front of the politician. The old goat got real indignant, insulted, I guess, because I didn't jump at the chance to go to bed with him, and he stormed out. Dan hit me so hard, my ears were ringing. Then he knocked me down a flight of stairs. All the petticoats I had on cushioned the fall, so I was just bruised and banged up some, no broken bones. I guess I got chicken then, because I started thinking about a lot of things that just aren't that important when you come down to it. I was afraid. I was frightened of Dan and the way he acted because I crossed him, and I was frightened what'd happen to me in a big town like New Orleans without any money. So...I did something stupid. For the most part, I started doing what Dan told me to do. That meant taking some fellows home with me once in a while. It was hard. It wasn't like I was a stranger to love, but I'd never done anything like that for money...." She paused and looked at me. She had an expression like, "Hell, maybe I'm telling him too much. Maybe he'll be like all the others."

"I got a big mouth, Santo. I hope I'm not talking out of turn."

I stared down at the matted straw, fidgeted and turned away. "I wanted to know about you."

We were both quiet for a minute.

"Anyway, things went along like that for a few months. Then this thing – actually a couple of things – happened that forced me to take a good hard look at the situation I'd gotten myself into. First, my brother came down from St. Louis looking for me. I don't know how he did it, because he didn't know about Little Rock and Sweet Home. I guess it was one big accident that he stumbled into that dance hall. I lied to him about what I was doing there and thought it'd keep him satisfied for a day or two until I could get rid of him. And I had to keep him from running into Dan.

"That was one of the worst weeks of life. Dan was on my tail. Charlie, my brother, was on my tail. Then Charlie got a telegram from home. My daddy, who'd put Charlie up to looking for me in the first place, had wired him that Mama died. Of course, Daddy said it was from a broken heart because of her poor, lost little girl. Christ, she was my stepmother! My real mother was long dead. Charlie was under Daddy's thumb, but he had his own ideas of getting me back to St. Louis. Like spying on me after I got off work. He went into a fit when he saw what was going on. If he hadn't been upset enough already, me working in a dance hall, now he was fit to be tied. I didn't realize right away that he'd found out till I discovered something he'd left on my dressing table. I'd just had a pretty rotten time with this Natchez gambler who had a mouth full of smelly, silver teeth. I was sitting there after he'd left, wanting to put a gun to my head and pull the trigger. You know what it's like, when you're drunk and miserable, and you happen to look up and find yourself staring in a goddamn mirror. How low could I get? I was about to find out.

"Right then, a fight started outside my door. I lived in the only room on the top floor of a ramshackle house at the end of Bourbon Street, so there wasn't anyone else to have to answer to at that time of night. Everybody else in the neighborhood was used to both white and black trash alike raising a ruckus and making enough noise to wake the dead. I opened the door, and Charlie fell in with Dan on top of him. It wasn't but a minute or two before Charlie got the upper hand. Charlie's a big, strapping boy, bigger than Dan. Before I knew it, Dan was lying there knocked cold, and Charlie was standing over me, breathing like a goddamn bull in a bullring, everything but smoke coming out of his nose. Blood was running down his face and chest. Charlie's got brown hair, but it was black with blood. And it only took me a few seconds to realize it wasn't his blood. He whirled away from me, reached outside the door onto the hall floor and picked up this big, black bullwhip. He shut the door real calm and came over to stand beside Dan. 'You whisper a goddamn word, you whore bitch, and I'll knock you cold!' He whispered it, but it sent chills down my spine. He looped the whip up over the center rafter of the ceiling, then started fooling with the other end of it. Suddenly, I figured out what he was doing. I was drunk, so it took me a minute. He was making a noose! A hangman's noose! He was slipping it around Dan's head when I lunged at him. He knocked me flat, and when I opened my eyes again, the whip noose was around Dan's throat. I jumped at Charlie one more time. He wasn't taking any chances. He knocked me down again and started tearing up the bedsheets. All the time that he was ripping up those dirty, filthy sheets, he was crying. With the raggedy cotton strips, he tied my wrists and ankles.

"When I came to, I was hogtied like that, and Dan had been strung up like he was a two-bit killer. Not that he was any saint, but he didn't deserve to be lynched by my crazy, fool brother. Charlie lay there on the floor, drinking up what was left of my liquor. I pretended to be out till I finally saw him go under. Then I struggled like a bitch in heat to get those knots untied before he came to. It took me almost two hours. I ripped my fingers raw while I stared at Dan's strangled, purple face and my dead drunk brother. At last I was free, and I got the hell out of there. And before I knew it, I was drifting across Mississippi and Alabama into Georgia."

My head was reeling at all this. "So what happened back there in Warm Springs, that little town in Georgia?"

"I lived comfortably there for a while. Tending bar, helping out the faro dealers. Till I realized they were running a crooked game and cheating green young 'uns and naïve tinhorns barely old enough to shave out of their life savings. This kid from Maryland shooting himself out in the street after he'd been fleeced – that was the last straw. I said the right thing at the wrong time and got the shit kicked out of me for my trouble."

After that, we didn't talk for a good half hour. She lay back down and stared at the car's ceiling. I didn't know what to say. But there was one thing I couldn't quite figure. Something she'd said had bothered her, and I couldn't understand why.

"What about what your brother had left on your dressing table? What was it? How come it bothered you so much?"

She got up again, then crawled over and sat close down to me. She gazed out at the passing countryside.

"It was a picture of me. A photograph of me the way I looked before I left St. Louis."

She paused.

"Yeah?"

"Well, the picture…" She was having trouble with that part for some reason. "In the picture…I'd been…a novice in a convent, the order of St. Ursuline. Two weeks after I'd taken my final vows as a nun, I ran away."

It took me a good while for all that to sink in. I didn't know too much about the Catholic religion, having been raised Baptist. My parents had thought all Catholics were in league with the Devil. Suddenly, it hit me. Something I'd heard about nuns and the gold bands they wore. Their wedding rings. And who they were supposed to be married to.

She'd really dropped a bombshell, and she knew it. She was staring at me, but I was still gazing out the open door. Hearing something like that on top of everything else made me realize that I must be in love with her. Instead of making me care less, that last thing about running away from the convent had intensified my feelings for her that much more. Not that I was her savior or anything, but I started thinking about her like maybe a kid would. An angel fallen from her cloud up in heaven and needing all the help she could to make it through this vale of tears. But I knew deep down she was no angel. She was a fallible creature made out of flesh and blood.

Then, all at once, she was crying her eyes out, rocking back and forth there on her knees with her face buried in her hands.

I moved over and put my arms around her frail shoulders and held her as tight and close as I could.

A hundred years from now, and what would it matter? I started thinking about that for some reason, about the future and how there'd probably be more comfortable and faster ways to travel, better roads to travel on, bigger and noisier towns to travel to and less distance between them.

And she and I would both be long dead. No more than dust. All the tragedy and terrible misfortune we'd both gone through...any profound thoughts you could conjure up about our lives and what it meant in the vast, ongoing scheme of things...why we'd met like we had. You tried to reason it out, you'd go crazy. I didn't want to try. I didn't want to head down that primrose path that only leads to a living, mortal hell on a cursed earth.

I laughed. Slowly, she straightened up, looking at me, some mixed-up, crazy quilt of feeling welling behind her eyes: first puzzled, then hurt, then angry. She backed away from me as I continued laughing. But I didn't stop. I couldn't. I fell on the vibrating floor of the cattle car and rolled and convulsed with laughter. Finally, through the tears running down my hot, flushed cheeks, I caught a glint of something else in her eyes.

Abruptly, she broke into it, too, and rocked her head back, slapping her thighs with the monstrously elaborate joke life had played on the both of us. Then, after a minute or two, we both let it subside. She got on her hands and knees, crept over to me and pressed her lips to mine, as hard as she could.

5

Not much else happened, except for us going on like that, talking and loving and watching out for any yard bulls when we slowed, maybe stopped for a few minutes at some whistlestop. We got to know each other pretty well in that day or so.

That country was something right then. It was the end of summer, and the trees and lakes, swamps and farmland we came through were beautiful as only the South can be at that time of year. Heading from a blistering summer into a muggy autumn. We went over a lagoon on one bridge a few miles outside of Montgomery that sticks in my mind as if it was yesterday. The water was a still purple sheet of reflection, a lavender mirror with weeping willows and cypresses poking up from the sunken shore. We came to a point where I could see gnarled, long-dead trees on the sandy, submerged bottom fifteen or twenty feet below. A flock of birds I don't know the name of got startled and took off, throwing the water into a shimmering rainbow of light.

Yeah, not much happened till a bit southwest of Hattiesburg, a sleepy little town in Mississippi you'd miss altogether if you sneezed.

When it happened, Lucy was asleep. I'd been lying there half-awake for about an hour, listlessly staring out through the slats of that charmed boxcar, hypnotized by the grey light of dawn.

All of a sudden, we were both slammed headfirst into the front end of the car. We'd hit something on the rail, I guess, because the whole train shook and rattled and seized-up in a spasm of destruction. It was like some giant had picked it up and tossed the entire line of cars off the tracks.

Neither of us were knocked cold, though I sprained my wrist, and Lucy sported a nasty cut on her chin. The car was still upright but perched at a precarious angle that made me uncomfortable. If either one of us leaned the wrong way, we'd topple it over on its side. I pressed Lucy against the floor to shift our weight. She looked at me, stunned.

"What the hell happened!"

I didn't answer. I was too busy trying to figure what was going on outside. The sliding door was pretty much wedged shut. The car creaked and moaned from buckling metal as I leaned forward, pushing back on the latch.

Outside, there was a lot of smoke and a hissing noise that was the locomotive's hot-as-hell engine spilling its guts on the rails.

I managed to get the door open to where there was enough room for us to squirm through. Then I heard something – something that I at first thought must've been the engineer and brakeman, whimpering from busted limbs. But the voices weren't the voices of hurting men. They were laughing, drunken voices. And, all at once, I realized what was going on.

There was the stamping of hooves, then gunshots. I hadn't seen one when we'd hopped aboard, but figured the train must've had a mail car. Because we'd been caught smack in the middle of a train robbery, plain as day.

There were more shots, I guess from the train people. I peered out between the splintered slats just in time to see the already bloodied engineer, brakeman and mail agents lined up on their knees and executed by a band of masked horsemen. There were six of the cutthroats, six of the most cold-blooded monsters I'd seen since Quantrill's days in Kansas.

I whispered to Lucy, "It's a hold-up, honey. If we sit tight and don't make a sound, I think everything'll be okay."

Then, right as if on cue, the car toppled over on its side.

Lucy cried out as she slammed into the already crumpled wall. I prayed to God that they hadn't heard her. I guessed that they probably hadn't, what with the crash walloping us into the hard ground.

Every bone in my body ached like crazy, and I could see that Lucy was pretty sore herself. I crept over to the trapdoor in the roof of the car. I couldn't hear anything from outside so had no idea what they were up to. Lucy crawled down next to me.

"Santo," she whispered, "I feel like my arm's broken." She was holding her left elbow. No bones were poking through bloody flesh, thank God, but I could tell that she was beside herself with pain. She couldn't move the fingers on her left hand at all.

Then I heard them next to the floor on the other end.

"It came out of here, I'm sure of it. Like a gal screamin' or somethin'."

"Or a stuck pig." Some phlegmy-sounding, thick-voiced bastard laughed.

I pressed a finger to my lips to make sure Lucy kept quiet and drew my Colt.

"Listen! What was that?"

"Yer goddamn imagination, Clem. There ain't nobody in there. You hearin' shit 'cause o'that twelve-year-old bitch you diddled last night in New Orleans." That set them roaring with laughter.

"Nah, I heard somethin'! I know it! Sure as the goddamn eyes on my face!" He was drunk and mad.

Whoever was in charge took over.

"Maybe Clem did hear somethin'. I got a feeling in my bones like I used to during the war when a bluebelly sniper was hangin' out of some nearby tree."

The voice sounded familiar, but the blood was pounding so loud in my ears I couldn't place it.

Then there was quiet. A stony silence that spooked the hell out of me because I didn't know if they had moved away from the car or not.

Lucy crept up close to my ear. "What are you going to do?"

I shrugged. She kissed me on the cheek and, in spite of the grave we'd dug for ourselves, I smiled. We must have waited a good twenty minutes before either of us moved again. There hadn't been a sound from outside except for the hissing of the cooling, dead engine.

"You think it's safe?" she whispered.

I gently twisted the handle of the ceiling hatch door. It sprang open from the pressure of its out-of-kilter lining.

Billows of smoke blew past the hole, hiding the tall grass growing beside the rails. I hesitated, then poked my head out. The bodies of the dead men lay face down on the gentle slope of the embankment about ten yards down the line.

"What's out there?"

"C'mon, " I reached back for her hand as I crawled the rest of the way through and stood up. She followed, as wary and as skittish as me. We took tentative baby steps down into the underbrush. Abruptly, there was a scraping sound from behind us, then the snorting of a horse. I leapt into the grass and brush, but whoever was out there with us was faster. They'd thrown a lariat, snagging Lucy tight and secure around her shoulders. She ducked too late, tried to slip the lasso from around her by prying her fingers beneath the rope. But the bastard yanked her backwards so she lost her footing and fell.

"Santo!"

I looked up as I landed in a bunch of jimson weed. There was a lone horsemen armed with a sawed-off shotgun, face hidden by a heavy burlap sack, perched atop the next overturned boxcar. His horse was nervous, prancing back and forth erratically on the splintered wood. But he had complete control over both the animal and Lucy.

All at once, there were others. They had the burlap hoods, too, and were armed with pistols.

Lucy whirled, pulling the rope taut with her good hand, trying with all her might to drag the killer off his mount, to no avail. He jerked as hard, as violently as he could, and she spun around, tripping into the dirt. With one massive, hairy paw, he reached down, clutched her around her wrist and hoisted her struggling hellcat body up beside him.

I had my Colt out by then and squeezed off three hasty shots. One winged him, and he dropped the shotgun. It was too bad that his pals had zeroed in on me. I ducked, but it was impossible to escape the hail of bullets that poured after me. I caught one in the shoulder, one in my left hand, and another grazed the small of my back. The force of the flying lead slammed me off my feet, rolled me down the incline into the dense brush. I tumbled for maybe ten yards because it was steep, and the grass and brush weren't strong enough to break my momentum.

I landed headfirst in a bubbling spring of warm, brackish water. When I came floating to the top, I couldn't see because of the hair in my eyes. I rolled over, and, with my good hand, swept the thick stuff away from my face. I kept my lids half-mast, partly because I didn't want them to see me still conscious, partly because I couldn't open them any further anyway.

"Look at the valiant hero!"

"He had a good life." That was the voice that was familiar again. Except there was something, low, guttural, muffled about it that didn't fit. Then again, he had a goddamn bag over his head.

They fired a few more shots at me from the top of the knoll, laughing the whole time. None of them connected, except for one that hit a cartridge in my gun belt. It fired, luckily exploding harmlessly into the water.

"Christ Almighty! Looky the water! It's as red as hell!"

"He's dead, floatin' in his own blood." They all laughed. Lucy suddenly screamed. I could barely see her blurred figure, kicking and scratching at their bulky, smothering forms.

The next thing I knew, they were gone. The sun was a lot lower in the sky, and I reckoned it was going to be getting dark any minute. I was lying half out of the water, my head resting on a bit of slimy moss that was drenched scarlet with the blood from my wounds. That scared me. There was hardly any pain with me lying still like that, but I knew I had to be hurt a lot worse than I felt. There was just too much blood. I was as weak as a kitten, and when I tried to move, a searing flame shot up from my hip to the top of my head.

Slowly, I inched my way up the embankment. It took me what must have been the best part of an hour just to make it half way. I took a breather then and listened real hard to see if there was anyone still around. Suddenly, a deep, throaty croaking started. I turned my face to stare into the face of a bullfrog as big as my hand. His stoic, uncaring expression made me laugh. Who gives a good goddamn about you? It made me think about Lucy, born for love in a godless world of monsters. And it made me mad.

I was going to find those sons-of-bitches that had taken her, and I'd make them pay, every last one of them. The anger, I guess, is what kept me going. I must have been as white as a sheet, because the blood just kept draining out of me.

When I reached the top of the slope, I was somehow able to stand up. I got my bearings and spotted a bunch of crates from an over-turned car, spilled a few yards away. Unfurled rolls of cotton and linen fabric in a rainbow of colors swathed the twisted iron rails like some drunk's attempt at a bandage. I shredded off a piece of lilywhite cotton and wrapped it, first around the hole on the side of my lower back, then the eruption of flesh in my left shoulder. Luckily, neither bullet had hit anything vital. They'd passed straight through. That made me happy for a minute. Suddenly, there was a stabbing in my left hand, and I doubled up. I fell face first on scattered pieces of yellow paper, the stocks and bonds the robbers had left behind. An iron safe lay upended, its twisted walls split open like a grotesque flower. I forced myself to stand again and gritted my teeth against the pain. Christ, I thought, if only I could get a drink.

I looked back down the line and saw the bodies of the men they had killed, flies buzzing over them in the stillness. It made me sick, and I had to put my one good hand over my mouth to keep from puking. Turning away so I didn't have to keep looking at all the blood helped a little. Everything in the war and the penitentiary rushed back at me, and I wondered why I was getting so squeamish all of a sudden. Maybe because of all the blood I had lost myself. Maybe being worried sick what those bastards were doing to Lucy.

I started to follow but stopped after only a few yards. I realized I still didn't have a horse. And I'd lost my Colt, probably had dropped it in the water when I was out cold.

I found another six-shooter right away, lying beside a dead brakeman. I picked it up and split open the chamber. Finding only two bullets left, I turned the body over and pulled his gunbelt off. There were fifteen bullets in it, so I slung it over my shoulder.

But how the hell was I going to follow them on foot after almost bleeding to death? The empty cattle car we'd been in gave me an idea. Maybe there were other cars with livestock actually in them. Christ, I was ready to ride a goddamn cow if I had to! I stumbled along the line almost to the end. It must have been the eleventh or twelfth car, the one just before the caboose, and it was lying on its side. I stopped at the splintered front and glimpsed streams of blood oozing out through the smashed slats. I could barely make out what was inside. It looked like three or four mules. Why anybody would bother to load a few jackasses into a perfectly serviceable cattle car was beyond me. But this was a hillbilly line headed through the heart of the Mississippi and anything was possible.

A horrible braying started up, and I realized one of them was still alive. I guess it must have heard me. Climbing onto the side of the car, I began yanking frantically at the door. Luckily, it hadn't gotten wedged shut and came open pretty easily.

He was caught between one of his dead brothers and the smashed wall. He stared at me with a crazy look in his eyes, a look that told me it wasn't going to be any piece of cake getting him to do what I wanted. I figured I'd better find a length of rope somewhere to use as a bridle and reins so he wouldn't run out on me as soon as I had him loose. Scores of broken crates that had been roped together littered both sides of the embankment. I tugged away a thick shank of the frayed stuff, then slung it around my neck – something I shouldn't have done so carefree. It hit my shoulder and shot a thunderbolt of fire up through my head that had me almost passing out again.

I closed my eyes, bending over slightly, and took several deep breaths. Then, impatient as hell, I yanked at the cracked slats. They split in two with little effort, and then I had the mule out. As soon as I had him onto the level ground, I noticed the shallow cuts on his right flank. He was so scared he didn't try to run at all. In fact, I had trouble getting him to move, period. He didn't like the makeshift reins I'd fashioned and kept spitting them out. I reckoned that being gentle with him was the best idea, so patted him on the head and talked to him in a soothing way. Finally, my gentle, insistent manner paid off, and he let me lead him down the slope to the water. I took the bridle out and let him have his fill, all the time stroking the back of his neck and purring affectionate nonsense in his ear. I quickly realized I had to get him away before he busted his gut. He didn't want to, but I kept nudging him back and forth, pushing and pulling, and it did the trick. When I climbed on top of him, he flinched, braying and trying to throw me, I guess because the one side of him was pretty sore. Then again, he was a goddamn mule. I did my best to keep off his scraped flank. At last, he figured I wasn't going to get off so settled down. I wheeled him around in the right direction, and we were off.

You might be thinking running off on a mule was a damn fool idea, but he was all that I had. I knew it was going to be slow. The whole bunch had already left us in the dust, so I supposed speed wasn't going to make much difference. I just kept hoping that Lucy could take care of herself as well as she'd made out to me in her stories.

The tracking I had learned during the war from a Cree Indian scout had never worked that well before. Now that I was nearly dead, floating in a reverie of delirium, everything I'd been taught, forgotten or hadn't understood because of my bullheaded stubbornness, took over. I was following the pack of them as easily as if they'd been a herd of buffalo stampeding through the brush.

It had already been dark for a couple of hours when their trail led back up to the rail line. I was dog-tired and achey, and I knew the mule didn't feel much better. But I wasn't going to rest. Not until either the mule or I gave out.

The dense forest fell away from the rails some, and with that break in the trees came more light. Moonlight. It was a full moon, and it started me remembering again, things I couldn't block out no matter how hard I tried.

There was the slow and steady clip clop of the mule's hooves on the rail ties, the crunch of the gravel beneath and every once in a while, the sound of locusts or the scurrying of some small animal in the shadows of the tall grass. A herd of cicadas broke out in a chorus of screeching, and my drowsiness left me. It, too, reminded me of many things, just as the moonlight did. The things that made my heart beat faster.

The cicadas brought back the tales of voodoo I'd heard, stories from superstitious freed men and women and white folk both. I recalled Eugenie, the old family cook and her stoop-shouldered, white-bearded mate, Pete. Pete with his perpetually crumbling corncob pipe. Those two sitting around the fire on a late October night, maybe Hallow's Eve, filling up a young boy's head with ghosts and goblins and zombie suicides buried at the crossroads who'd return from the grave on certain days to take vengeance on their mortal enemies.

My mind wandered – Millie and mother and the men I'd known in the war. Suddenly it hit me, the voice of the main masked bandit. But I still couldn't place exactly who it was. There had been too many men, too many faces. Not that many friends, though, and it worried me because the voice had been the voice of a friend.

If I hadn't kept on bleeding, maybe it would have come to me. If not for the bandages, I would've been dead in a few hours. As it was, I thought I would probably last a couple of days. The holes in me were throbbing like crazy. I wracked my brain to remember the roots and leaves Eugenie used to collect to make poultices. Since the bullets had passed through the wounds, all that I had to worry about was treating the raw, swollen flesh.

That's when I felt the little box in my pants pocket, Lucy's salve. I pulled it out, and sure enough, that's what it was. I couldn't for the life of me recall when she'd handed it over. I took another whiff, and the pungent smell gave me a good idea what was in it – elder, comfrey, slippery elm with maybe a small pinch of foxglove. I fingered out a small glob and smeared it under both sides of the bandage on my shoulder. It stung so badly, I almost fell off the mule. Patting it into the graze on my lower back made me double up with pain, and I clutched one of the mule's ears to keep my balance. It threw him into a fit of braying panic, but I managed to hold on.

It dawned on me that using the stuff was making me more delirious. Again I pitched sideways, nearly swooning, but caught myself just as I was falling. Hurting like it did, I figured the stuff sure as hell must've been doing some good. I thought that I might have just covered myself for warding off the gangrene. I slipped some more of the sticky yellow under the bandage on my palm.

Suddenly I couldn't stay upright anymore. I slumped forward, breathing heavily, heart pounding like a sledgehammer, then dropped my head and chest on the mule's neck. He stopped. I whispered in his ear and shook the reins so he'd go on, and he took a few tentative steps as slow as molasses. It was like that for about a hundred yards. I don't know why, but I started to thinking maybe the bunch that had grabbed Lucy had called it quits for the night and were holed up somewhere in the vicinity. That spooked me, that they might have set up camp somewhere very near, that we could suddenly plow straight into them. The whole idea made me more lightheaded then ever, and I got so dizzy I nearly dropped off again. I tugged on the rope, and he gave me an indignant snort at the herky-jerky nature of our travel.

As soon as I'd been stopped for a couple of minutes, I heard voices. They were coming from another hundred yards or so off, carrying through the trees and the marsh. Sure enough, my instincts had been right.

I did my best to sit up straight and steer the mule in their general direction. We drew to a halt when we were pretty close, in fact, maybe just a little too close for comfort. Even in my half-conscious state, I was alert enough to realize what could happen if the mule started his braying during the middle of the night. But I was too faint to do anything about it. I slipped off with a heavy thud, the rope reins still tangled in my good hand and wrapped them around the rotting carcass of a felled oak.

In all honesty, I don't quite know what it was that I expected to be able to do. I was as weak as a kitten and sure not in any shape to stand up against even one, let alone all of them. Lying there flat on my back, I immediately drifted into a deep sleep.

6

I don't know how long I lay there, but I came fitfully awake at the sound of gunfire. The sky was grey in the east, so I knew dawn wasn't far off. The echoing report of both rifles and pistols stopped as quickly as it began, a flurry of staccato shots, then nothing. The mule did his hee-haw routine on cue, and I clapped my hand over his mouth to muzzle him. He snapped his teeth trying to bite my fingers, but I was too fast for him, giving him a solid rap across the nose with the gun barrel. There was the stampeding of hooves. Not a lot of horses, probably only two of them, running in the opposite direction from me. And then that sound was gone, too.

I had no idea what it all meant but was set on finding out. Unfortunately, my body had other plans. As soon as I tried to stand up, a great whooshing roar flooded through my head, and I nearly passed out. When I could focus again, I was staring at the transparent skin of my good hand, a deathly pale white showing just how much blood I had lost.

I made it to my feet again and, leading the mule on foot through the dense brush, I headed in the direction of the shots. The brush thinned out at the top of a rise. On the other side was a shallow, spread-out ravine composed mostly of mud and shattered rock. When I didn't pick up on any movement, I pressed closer to the lip of the ridge.

It was some kind of abandoned mine site. A few craggy holes, mine shafts I suppose, shored up with rotten timbers pocked the opposite side.

The first thing I saw that didn't seem quite right were the pools of red scattered in several depressions in the valley floor. Then I saw the bodies lying prone, face down, looking about as dead as you can get. So the red was blood. And the bodies were the bodies of the men who had held up the train. Except there were only five of the mud-spattered corpses – there'd been six men at the train. And there was no sign of Lucy at all.

I climbed on the mule, spurring him with my heels, and we started down towards the bloody scene. Passing the drowned campfire, I spotted an overturned coffee pot lying a few inches from the stiff, clutching hand of one of the men.

I reined in on the mule and squinted up at the overcast sky. It was already drizzling and looked like a good-sized downpour before the end of the day. All of a sudden, the mule brayed, and there was a scraping sound from a few yards ahead.

I lowered my head to stare into the crazy eyes of one of the "dead" robbers. What I saw in his eyes was a shock, not because of what it was, but because it was so damn clear. The dreams of a lifetime – in his case unimaginative dreams about easy money, loose women and corrosive rotgut – were spilling out of him, dimming and dying with each convulsive breath. His face was the worn face of a no longer tough, middle-aged man, his hair receding to reveal a bald skull covered with grease and ash. Stretched out on his stomach, his legs were spreadeagled behind him, his arms clamped tightly together, his head raised with palsied exertion. Then I saw what he was holding in both of his shaking, blood-smeared hands. A gun was pointed directly at me. I jerked on the rope reins as he squeezed the trigger, and the mule caught the echoing blast full in the face. The animal crumpled, front legs first, throwing me into the mud scant inches from the dying thief. My gun already in my hand, I pressed the barrel to his temple and slapped his gun away. But I didn't want to kill the son-of-a-bitch yet, not until I'd found out about Lucy.

"What happened?"

He gave me a stupid smile, laughed and coughed up globs of coagulating blood.

"He kil't us! Thash wha' happned! Jimmy got a lil' smartmouth an' he did no' like it, so he drew his gun – " he coughed violently again, " – an' he kil't Jimmy! He kil't all o' us!"

"What about the girl?"

He laughed again, then his eyes glazed over, and he was dead.

I knelt there in the mud, dazed by the sight of so much blood. Big watery ponds of it around each member of the gang. He, whoever he was, was a brutal bastard. And he'd taken Lucy with him.

I was right back where I'd started. The mule was dead, and I didn't see any of the gang's horses lingering in the vicinity. The dirty butcher had either taken them with him or scattered them off into the woods. I was banking on the latter. I hadn't heard but two horses after the gunfire and, if he had just scattered the rest, a couple would undoubtedly wander back that way in due time.

It started to rain, and I quickly searched the camp to see if they'd left behind any food. There was about half of a charred rabbit still skewered above the ruins of the campfire. I grabbed it and ducked into one of the nearby mine shafts to escape the deluge. It came down in buckets all day. And as the day wore on well into the morning, then past noon, the blacker the sky became.

I felt like that sky was a mirror of my insides. The holes in me didn't feel so bad anymore because Lucy's salve was working as good as any poultice. The few bites of rabbit I'd had to eat had even made me feel a little stronger. I probably should have been considering myself lucky. But I was despairing of ever being able to see Lucy again, at least alive.

When night came on, the rain let up some. What happened next, though, was far worse than any rainstorm. I didn't notice it right away because I'd been dozing on and off ever since dusk. It wasn't until a bloodcurdling howl split the quiet that I knew I was not alone. I'd had myself propped up against a pile of sand and smashed rock right at the mouth of the shaft so I'd be able to catch any horse coming back into the area. When the howling came, I sprang forward onto my stomach, the Remington .44 in hand. I hunkered down close to the gravel and peered across the ravine.

There was a little sliver of moon out, so it wasn't pitch black. What I saw froze me up inside. A pack of wolves was frantically scurrying about sniffing at the corpses. Before long, they tired of lapping at the bloody pools of water and attacked the bodies themselves. I didn't want to start firing into them unless I had to. There were too many and, if I missed at all, I could very easily run out of ammunition. Then I'd be a goner for sure. So I sat tight and waited.

There were at least ten of them, and they were having a feast. They ripped away the raggedy clothes first, then tearing and rending with their iron jaws, pulled off big strips of flesh. Chunks of human meat would fly into the air from one violent savaging, and the wolf closest would catch it before it hit the ground, gobbling it down in the most gruesome, gluttonous fashion.

I did my best to keep from throwing up the meager bit of nourishment I'd taken. But I had to keep still, and I had to keep watching. If I'd made a move farther back into the cave, or given myself the luxury of a fit of retching, the whole bunch could have been on me at once. And I wouldn't have had a chance. After emptying the six-shooter, there would be no time to reload.

I had to use my frail will power. After about half an hour or so of their bloodglut, I think my eyes must have glazed over.

Then as quickly as they had come, they were gone. I waited for almost an hour after they'd slunk off before I crawled back deeper into the recesses of the cave. When the darkness and relative protection was finally mine, I passed out into a deep, restful sleep.

The next morning I woke to a hot wind whistling through the tunnel. Groggily, I crept on all fours to the mouth of the cavern. It was still overcast, but I could see the sun behind the clouds and reckoned it to be about noon. It was hard to believe I'd slept so long. I felt good considering what I had been through. The bulletholes weren't gangrening up, so I slapped on some more of Lucy's salve.

Then something I heard made me sit bolt upright, perking my ears to be sure I wasn't mistaken. And there she was, a weather-beaten roan, saddled and all, picking her way through the chuckholes and gnawed-clean bone leavings of the dead men. How she'd stayed in the area what with the wolves and the rain was a mystery to me. I had just about given up hope that any of the horses would be back.

I knew I'd have to play it careful. One wrong move on my part could spook the hell out of her, and she'd be a mile away before I knew what hit me. On a hunch, I whistled to her. Immediately she pricked her ears and turned in my direction. But she didn't come any closer. I made clucking sounds with my tongue. She dipped her head down to a clump of grass, nibbling hungrily at what little stubble was there. As I tentatively stepped out of the shaft, she raised herself up and stared at me.

I could tell what her tiny brain was thinking. She didn't know me by either sight nor smell, so straightaway I was suspect. But I wasn't making any threatening gestures, and she seemed to be sitting tight to see what I was going to do next. Maybe I was giving her more credit than she was due, though she had to be a little bit smart to have kept clear of the wolfpack all night long. I kept it up with the friendly noises, then suddenly she spooked and started backing away. I froze.

"It's okay, honey. I don't want to hurt you. I'm the only one here. C'mon, be a good girl."

I wished I had had a carrot or apple or piece of sugar cane to make her want to believe me. I took small, short steps, walking down a slight incline of rock to get to her, and saw she wasn't happy about having to look up at me. Then again, maybe it was the smell of flesh beginning to putrefy that was getting her so riled. The whole patch of ground right there in front of the mine shaft stunk like hell. It was just too bad I couldn't do anything about it. I didn't like the smell either. What with my empty stomach and all, it was making me woozy.

I jumped, grabbing and latching onto her reins trailing in the mud. She bucked, rearing on her hind legs, but I held on fast. She was a real devil, that roan. I had to concentrate every bit of my strength in that one good hand, and it wasn't much. I wasn't healed up, not by a long shot, and she just about pulled my arm out of its socket yanking back and forth like she did. If I'd slipped, if I'd let her go, I would have kissed my chances goodbye.

Right when I was weakening, when I thought that I just couldn't hold on any longer or keep out of the way of her hooves, she settled down. The tension in the reins abruptly slackening took me by surprise, and I fell flat on my face in the mud. Luckily my good hand wasn't paying attention and held onto the reins nice and tight.

She just stood there, looking at me. A couple of minutes went by before I got my bearings and was on my feet again. Instead of giving her a good belt in the mouth, I patted her long nose. She was a gift from heaven, and I wasn't going to take her for granted, not for a second. Painfully, I bent over, making sure her saddle was secure underneath, then I climbed on top of her. She whinnied, nodding her head like she was glad to finally find someone who could lead her out of that horrible, stinking mess.

I was on their trail like that for a good two days. Where I was or was going to end was a mystery to me. I thought, at one point, I might have crossed the border into Louisiana, but I wasn't sure.

The holes in me hadn't gotten any worse, though I was getting weaker from nothing to eat and the loss of blood. The roan was doing fairly well, considering. She had warmed up to me after only a few hours, undoubtedly relieved to be rid of her previous cruel masters.

Without warning, we ran right into a town. It was called Picayune and was made up of two or three streets about a half mile in length running parallel to each other. Still in Mississippi, I guessed it to be probably an hour or so from New Orleans proper.

Before I did anything else, I wanted to find myself a doctor. A young raggedy girl sitting in the dirt in front of the main hotel told me where to go. The doctor called himself Emil Marleybone and had his modest, cluttered office above a feed store next door to the livery stable. I turned the roan over to a slow-witted boy with half his teeth missing and watched him for a few moments as he took off her saddle and blankets and started to feed her. Once I was sure she was okay, I climbed the fragile outside stairs to the doctor's office.

Luckily, he was in. As I said, the office was cluttered; small and filled to bursting with medical supplies, empty whiskey bottles and other assorted old junk. Dr. Marleybone described the junk as antiques. I found him sleeping on a sagging, torn-up couch with his face hidden beneath a newspaper.

I slapped my good hand against the soles of his boots, and he shot bolt upright, shouting declarations of loyalty to the Confederacy, then upon seeing me, slightly less eloquent curses and oaths.

"What the hell you want?"

I pointed to the makeshift bandages that covered my wounds.

He rubbed a grimy thumb and forefinger on the bridge of his nose, then slipped on a pair of smeary-lensed spectacles.

"It appears that you may have had a disagreement with the wrong kind of gentleman, young lad."

"I suppose you could call it that. Just don't call me 'young lad.'"

He blinked at my admonition and smiled. "I take it you possess the finances to have me address you as something different? Something more appropriate and salutary to your exalted station in life?"

That threw me. It was the first time in several days that I'd had to think about money. I searched my pockets while Marleybone smirked knowingly.

"Ahem. I thought as much. Nothing to back up your peacockery!"

With a self-satisfied smile, I pulled a damp, crumpled dollar bill from my pants to prove him wrong. Eyes widening, he snatched it out of my hand, jumped up, then pushed me roughly down onto the lounge where he'd been napping. He knelt before me.

"Let's see now, young lad – I mean, young man. Let me see exactly the extent of the damage." He gingerly picked away the bandage on my shoulder and suddenly held his nose with his other hand. "Ye Gad! Your wound smells like the back room in Jeremiah's Funeral Parlor!"

I made a face.

He rubbed the yellow paste that covered the entry and exit holes with a dirty finger. "What in Jehovah's name be this?"

"A salve a friend of mine gave me. A poultice."

"Hmm, an old Indian remedy, no doubt. Well, young fellow, you are very lucky – so far." He pulled away the other bandages with a care and a delicacy contradictory of his blustery manner. The least of my wounds, the graze along my back and side, hurt the worst. A whole sheet of fire shot through the flesh as the bloody rags came away.

He winced. "Sorry, my friend." Then he stood up. "You are very, very fortunate. You seem to have lost a vast quantity of blood. But you've also obviously stopped the blood flow at a crucial point. In other words, before you could expire. I shall proceed to clean and dress your unfortunately affected areas."

He ripped open a wooden cabinet that had all its varnish worn away and proceeded to ransack it, throwing various items over his shoulder into a long neglected corner of the room. Producing a slender vial of a milky blue liquid from behind a row of dusty jars, he gave off a shout of triumph. Eyes gleaming, he wobbled back across the room, navigating the obstacle course of tables, chairs, books and garbage with nary a glance. He grabbed a tangled wad of cloth, a needle and a spool of surgical thread from a low box beside the lounge.

"Might as well stitch up these holes for you while I'm at it, son. They'll heal up quite a bit faster."

Picking up the washbasin from his desk, he threw the standing liquid out the window without a second thought, then replaced it from a pitcher of comparatively fresh water. His washing of hands would've been a comical ceremony to watch if he'd been planning to treat anybody other than me. As it was, his whole slightly drunken demeanor was making me have my doubts. While he was finishing up his meager preparations, I sank back down on the cushions and thought, what the hell, he couldn't make things much worse than they were already.

"Here we go!" He was sitting on the edge of the couch, trying to thread the glistening, curved stitching needle. I looked at his five o'clock shadow, the holes in his coat and dirty hat, his squinty-eyed countenance deep in concentration, and burst out laughing. I guess I shouldn't have because, at least about himself, he didn't have the greatest sense of humor. He turned on me indignantly, his pride smarting.

"What strikes you so humorous, young lad!"

I wiped the grin off my face and shook my head. Christ, it hurt like hell to laugh anyway.

He shrugged and, with a decidedly cruel relish, dug in. I yelped.

"Shhh! Here, take this." One hand still stitching me up, he used the other to offer a carafe of rye from its place on the floor. I bubbled it for nearly half a minute. That, coupled with the no-food proposition of the last couple of days, nearly put me out. I don't remember much about that next hour or so, except it took at least that long for him to finish up his work on me. When he was done, he took a long pull on the rye, then winked.

"You're on that golden road to recovery now, son. In a day or two you'll be as good as new. But! And this is a very important 'but'... get yourself some good rest."

"I...I...don't have anywhere to stay."

He frowned and rubbed his chin thoughtfully with a gnarled, arthritic hand. Noticing for the first time the stiff, curled fingers, I wondered at his skill in patching me up. He'd actually done a pretty damn good job.

"Well, well, well. An itinerant. A transient cowpoke. On your way west to the promised land, no doubt?"

"I ain't no cowboy."

For some reason that made him laugh, and he slapped his leg as his whole body rocked with mirth. When his fit of laughter finally subsided, he grew instantly sober.

"Very well, my friend. And you obviously have no friends of your own besides me in this town. I think I can fix up a room for you at the hotel. I don't usually do this, but if you pay me instead of that buffoon of a clerk, I'll get you a sizable discount."

"How much?"

He did some mental figuring while staring up at the ceiling. "Ahem. Let me see now. Hmmm, hmmm. Let's see...two dollars...for two days."

I didn't know what the going price was for anything anymore so just nodded.

"Good. You stay here and rest, and I'll be back directly."

I handed him the money, and he sprang off the couch. He was out the door in a flash.

While he was gone, I just lay there, too drained to do much else, too relieved at receiving "professional" medical treatment to be concerned over the specter of Lucy's whereabouts and welfare.

I let my eyes wander about the room and my gaze fell on a hanging skeleton chained to the ceiling by the door. It had a Sioux headdress draped over its skull.

For some reason I hadn't noticed it before.

Suddenly Marleybone was back, huffing and puffing with the exertion and exhaling smoke rings from a newly acquired cigar. He immediately caught me staring at the dusty old collection of bones.

"You've met ole Scarhead, have you?"

"Scarhead?"

"Yes, that's his real name. A notorious Sioux chief. Too notorious even for most of the Sioux. A renegade to his own people, renowned for kidnapping white women and mutilating their homesteader husbands." He saw my bafflement. "Oh, this didn't happen around here. Scarhead's from up Kansas way. He was captured by our cavalry in 1869 and executed by hanging the very same year. I picked up his skeleton from an enterprising resurrectionist fellow in early '70."

"Resurrectionist?"

"In common parlance, a grave robber. He supplies the medical profession with bodies. For anatomical purposes." He saw my revulsion at the ghoulish revelation and, once again, became indignant.

"For study, my boy. To help doctors help poor unfortunates like yourself. What other guide to the corporeal mortal shell do we have but the human body itself? This fellow Scarhead certainly has been of more service to humanity and even his own red brothers now in death than he ever was in his life!"

I tried to sit up. Amazingly enough I was successful.

"Easy, young fellow." He patted me on the shoulder.

"You got me the room?"

"Yes. Clean sheets and a calm, quiet atmosphere to aid in your recuperation." He helped me up on my feet, and I at once reeled with the effort. He braced me, though, and in a scant few seconds my head was clear. It was then that I realized how hungry I was. A hollow pit yawned in my stomach.

"Tell me, doc, this hotel have food?"

"Why, yes, my boy, an excellent restaurant saloon downstairs next to the registration desk in the lobby."

"Good."

"Yes, that would be a very prudent measure, the taking of solid nourishment…" He winked a sly wink, and his boozy breath swept over me, "…as opposed to liquid sustenance."

We stumbled unsteadily across the room together. He helped me on with my jacket, and I stuck my Remington back in my belt. I turned to the door only to come face-to-face with Scarhead. Up close, I could see a moldy cigar butt sticking from between his teeth.

"Tell me, Doc, why did they call him Scarhead?"

He took off his hat and pointed to his own balding pate, running his palsied fingers back and forth. "He had scars all over the top of his shaved head. I suppose it was some sort of unhealthy purification ritual, an obsession of his. That's how the story goes. Scared the hell out of everyone, even his own warriors."

"I bet." I shook Marleybone's hand, and he groaned at the slight pressure. "Sorry, Doc."

"That's all right, boy. I've a nasty case of arthritis. Nothing can be done, so I just have to live with it." He smiled miserably.

Then I was out the door. As an afterthought, I turned back on the landing,

"You haven't happened to see a dark-haired young lady come into town the last day or two? Probably in almost as bad a condition as me?"

He looked troubled. "No…no," he said at last, shaking his head. "I haven't. Sorry." He quickly shut the door.

I thought he'd reacted strangely to the question, but I didn't know if he was lying or if it was just my befuddled imagination.

The hotel was a rundown, unlooked-after affair that gave the lie to its gingerbread house exterior. The unshaven clerk was draped over the registration desk, head resting peacefully on folded arms and snoring up a storm. Stepping into the lobby, the rotten floorboards creaked beneath me, and he came awake.

"Can I help you?"

"Doc Marleybone was over here about a room."

A puzzled look came over his face, exaggerated by his cockeyed stare.

"Oh, yes." He turned the registration book around for me. "Doc's already taken care of everything. All you have to do is sign in."

I picked up the pen and jotted down an alias. "That it?"

He nodded. "How long you think you'll be with us?"

I shrugged, took the key and headed upstairs.

After seeing the lobby, the closet-sized chamber with the peeling, yellowed wallpaper was about what I'd expected. The large double four-poster bed was the sole concession to luxury, but it made up for that sin by taking up the entire room. Flimsy torn curtains fluttered before a narrow open window directly opposite the door.

I flopped down on the lumpy mattress wondering where my next piece of change was going to come from. I pulled a few crumpled bills from my pants pocket. Five dollars left.

Then Lucy came into my thoughts. Her trail was still plenty hot. In fact, I figured there was a better than even chance that both her and the masked man were right there in Picayune. Before I could mull it over for too long, I fell fast asleep, a deep restless slumber filled with threatening dreams.

The first dream was about Millie and Lucy both. They knew each other and had me camped out in a luxury suite, the bridal chamber of some swank hotel. There was blood-red velvet all over the place – on the furniture, beds, walls, even the floor. The only thing wrong was Lucy black and blue from a beating and Millie with those bleeding bulletholes I'd helped to put in her back in Louisville. I woke up in a cold sweat. But before I could even sit up, I was out cold again.

Then came the real clincher: Lucy naked there in bed with me, showering me with kisses and gentle caresses. We made love, and it was nothing but the purest sweetness and light. Out of nowhere, a giant menacing shadow fell across the both of us, and we were suddenly riddled with caustic, burning lead.

I awoke with a start, breathing heavily, my heart pounding so hard I thought it was going to give up and quit.

As soon as that subsided, the hunger hit me again with sledge-hammer force, and I had to hold back a fit of retching from the sour emptiness coursing through my gut.

I locked up the room and headed downstairs. When I reached the lobby, I saw through the open front door that the sun was already setting. The clumsy, ne'er-do-well clerk fumbled with matches at the lamps along the wall.

I found my way into the saloon. A sullen, fat-assed bartender grudgingly took my order of steak, greens and baked potato, then disappeared into a cubbyhole that was the kitchen entrance.

There were three men separate from each other jauntily posed along the bar.

A gal in a dancehall dress sat at the piano, half-heartedly fiddling with the keys. It was dark in there, illuminated by a few lanterns spaced on the wall, one lone overhanging battery of lamps and a solitary candelabra poised directly in the center of the bar counter.

The bartender returned almost immediately with my food. One of the men drinking turned around to see who the grub was for. When he saw me, a shocked expression seemed to come over his face. I tried not to pay any attention to him and dug into my supper. After a couple of minutes, he started over to the table with a bottle.

His face was a craggy mass of age lines, pockmarks and scars, and it took me a few minutes to recognize him. The huge Stetson that shadowed the top half of his face didn't help any. When he'd almost gotten to the table and the palm of my hand was resting on the butt of the Remington just out of sight, it hit me. Leroi Cameron. One of the only friends I'd had in my whole sorry outfit during the war. Seeing him again, I noticed a poisonously cruel frenzy deep in his eyes that gave me the willies. But remembering the old Leroi I'd known so well, my favorable memories of him, and his casual manner as he sauntered lazily across the floor, put me at ease. This conflicting set of emotions became even clearer when he opened his mouth.

"Hello, Santo. Long time no see."

He was the masked man from the train. The bastard who'd massacred his own men and kidnapped Lucy. Against my better judgment, I loosened my grasp on the Remington and laid both hands on the table.

He laughed a crazy drunken laugh and pulled his Colt from its holster, barrel first.

"I got a toothache."

I couldn't figure out what he was doing until he smacked himself in the mouth with the heavy butt of the gun and spat out a gold tooth. Crimson running off of it, he let the tooth lay there on the table between us, picked up his whisky glass and held it just below his whiskered jaw to let the blood drain. He bolted the sloppy, sickening mess, swallowing noisily and slammed the glass back down.

"You son-of-a-bitch, Santo!" He picked the shiny tooth between a blackened thumb and forefinger. "You know how much your life is worth? This much." He threw the tooth across the room. The other men at the bar didn't even look over at us. He was worse than during the war… a lot worse. I remembered when we'd both been whoring in Montgomery right after a lot of fighting, both of us feeling so dead inside. We hadn't had to mention a word to each other. We knew what was deep in each other's hearts. And it had been sad. The girls we were with had seemed dead, too. Deader than dead. In my drunken stupor, I'd wondered what business so many "dead" people had carousing in one place together.

Now there was no use asking him what he was talking about. I didn't really have to because I felt that I knew anyway. Why he was even bothering to talk to me and not plugging me full of holes was anybody's guess. Maybe it was for old time's sake. Maybe it was because of Lucy. Maybe she'd softened him up somehow.

I took a long swig from the bottle.

"How long you been at this, Leroi?"

"What?" His eyes were wild with pathetic self-pity, and every bit of humor was dripping with corrosive poison.

"You know what I mean. I'm lucky I'm still alive. I just got back from the doctor."

He roared with laughter that turned into a fit of coughing. "That Marleybone! Ha, ha, ha, you lucky you still alive, boy. Hell, Santo, I'm more of a doctor with this," he waved his gun, "than he is with all his shit."

I was getting sick of his cocky bullshit. "What've you done with Lucy?"

That stopped him cold. He just looked at me for a good couple of minutes, hardly breathing, not saying anything. He stared back down into his bloody glass and the drops of red that dotted the uneven tabletop before him.

"What'd you do? Kill her?"

He looked up and wagged his head to say no. "She's ...she's really something, ain't she?"

I didn't answer.

He got impatient. "Yeah, you bastard, she's okay. What do you think I do, Santo? Go around shooting women, just for the hell of it?"

He was angry but it didn't register much with me. It was an act, just like everything else was with him. He hadn't been that way, not during the first year or so of the war. He hadn't been so hopeless, so brittle, so downright not giving a damn about anything until Atlanta had blazed into cinders before his very eyes.

Famished, I shoveled the food into my mouth. I sure wasn't going to let him stop me. It was pretty good steak. Tough, but then I suppose a fried piece of shoe leather would've been appetizing to me.

"Why'd you bump off all your partners there at the mineshaft?"

He didn't answer, just stared into his drink in a stupor.

I finished off the steak. And, after a few more minutes, the greens and potatoes were gone, too.

"Why'd you shoot me?"

He looked me in the eye as I pushed the greasy plate away.

"Wanna see her?"

Something in the way he said it, so sheepish and unsure of himself, made me want to say "no". But he was up and moving to a door in the back. He looked over his shoulder as he wobbled into the shadows. "C'mon, goddamn it. I'm doing you a goddamn favor. And it'd sure be nice if you appreciated it."

I got up with new strength, I reckon from the first square meal I'd had in days, and followed him through the door into a dimly lit room.

There she was with her back to me, hunkered down on her haunches with three men, a pair of dice rattling like a couple of tiny bones inside her hand. She let them go against the wall, calling the dice as she saw them fall. "Seven-eleven."

As soon as she called it, she stopped cold, frozen up, and I could see the hackles rising on the back of her neck. She whirled around, staring at me stupidly, her face flushed with drink, her eyes dull and lusterless, and her left arm twisted and held close to her as if she was in pain.

7

I couldn't utter a word. I turned my back on her and walked right out
the door, walked through the saloon throwing a few coins on the table
for my supper, then making it with a lot of difficulty through the lobby
and up the stairs to my room.

It felt as if she'd cut me up worse than all the bullets Leroi and
his gang had pumped into me, worse than all the goddamn bullets and
sabers that had scarred me during the war. It choked me up because I
couldn't figure it. It was too much for me to understand, and it put me
out into a deep, dreamless sleep.

I awoke with her naked there in the darkness clutching at me,
caressing my face and whispering a bunch of stuff I couldn't make
out, partly because I was still drunk and partly because she was, too.
It was black as pitch in the room. Her sweaty forehead pressed against
my cheek and her convulsive fingers moving against me were all that I
knew of her.

"You don't know how horrible it was, Santo. I wanted to die.
They all took their turns with me. Then he went nuts and killed
every one of them. He dragged me through the mud that was more
blood than mud, and the next thing I knew we were here in Picayune."

Then the tears came. She wept, clinging to me, showering me
with kisses.

"Oh, Santo, I thought you were dead. I thought that they'd murdered you. Ever since I last saw you lying in that bloody pool I've wanted to die."

Even though I could barely see her, I looked her in the eye for the first time since downstairs. "You didn't act like you wanted to die shooting craps in that back room."

She ignored that, sinking her head down low, crying into my chest. "Santo, I love you so. I thought I'd never, ever, ever see you again."

She held onto me tight, and her body was wracked with the sobbing. I didn't know if I believed her or not. She'd undoubtedly had her hands full since I'd last seen her, just trying to stay alive, using whatever trick or con she could to get Leroi to give her a bit more play in that invisible noose he had around her neck. One look at Leroi told me she had him wrapped around her little finger. And he wasn't the kind of fellow that just any ole girl could do that to. Maybe he was as in love with her as I was. Because I was still in love with her. I suppose it didn't matter much what she said. It scared the hell out of me that I felt that way. It's surely the fastest route to the graveyard I know of, being in love with a gal who's maybe no good, so in love it doesn't matter what she does or has done because you'd still go to the ends of the earth for her.

But her tears and what she was telling me, about how much she loved me, I had this gut feeling that all of it was genuine. It wasn't a show for my benefit. And I couldn't imagine her being a good enough actress to play the same part to Leroi and have him believe it.

"Leroi's in love with you."

She raised up some and stared at me with a question in her eyes.

"Well, isn't he?"

She slowly nodded.

"How'd you manage that?"

She was ashamed. "Once we were clear of the old mining camp, I quit fighting. I don't mean I went to bed with him. I've been stalling him. But I knew he meant business after he massacred his whole bunch."

"Why'd he do that?"

"He went into a rage when he came back from scouting the trail and found them screwing the living daylights out of me. That wasn't the only reason, though. The $30,000 from the train helped make his trigger-finger itchy, too."

"$30,000?"

"Yeah." She stopped, puzzled. "He knew you. You used to be... friends."

"During the war. I haven't seem him since."

"It started bothering him that they'd shot you like that and left you for dead. I didn't help him feel any better about it."

"So how're you going to get away from him? Have you thought about that?" I suppose I sounded bitter because she looked hurt.

She shook her head.

"Does he know you're up here with me right now?"

"He's too drunk to care. He's passed out in the room down at the end of the hall."

Suddenly disgusted, I turned away from her. Even though I believed how she felt about me, I wasn't so sure she was telling the truth about how far she'd gone with him. I knew Leroi well enough to know he wouldn't shoot a woman he fancied in cold blood just because she wouldn't come across. But her denial was too pat, a bit too easy. Obviously for my benefit.

"You aren't mad at me, are you Santo?"

I kept quiet.

"Santo..." she was whispering softly in my ear.

"You haven't been sharing his bed?"

"Only to sleep in. Nothing else." All at once, she changed from conciliatory to proud. "Hell! What do you think I am anyway? A goddamn – "

She didn't say it because she saw the look in my eyes. We both remembered her story about her brother and her pimp in New Orleans. She sat up, hitting one of the bedposts as hard as she could. "Christ! I don't give a good goddamn! Don't believe me if you don't want to."

I reached out and touched her bare shoulder to let her know it was okay. She felt the bandage on my hand for the first time and gently folded both her hands over it, pressing it to her breasts. "Oh, darling, how are you?"

"I'm okay. The doctor next door patched me up."

"Where'd they get you?"

She let go of my hand long enough to light the candle on the night table. The light showed her where. She winced, staring at my shoulder and side, traced her fingers softly across the dressings.

"Are you in pain?"

I shook my head. "That salve you left in my pocket pulled me through. I might be gangrened up real good now if it hadn't been for that foul-smelling stuff."

She started crying again, but quietly without any loud, theatrical boo-hooing to impress me. Tears rolled down her cheeks and fell on my chest.

"How about you, Lucy? That arm's all bruised and swollen."

She glanced down at it absentmindedly, then back up at me. "Doc Marleybone looked at it. Just a sprain. He had me wearing a bandage yesterday, but it itched too much."

I tenderly took hold of both her hands and pulled her down on top of me.

8

"You know, he's good friends with the sheriff here. Probably paying him off."

She lit the candle again, and I wondered what the hell time it was. I wondered what he was doing, how drunk he really was, and if he was liable to burst in on us all of a sudden, guns blazing.

"We can leave before sun up, be long gone before he knows what hit him."

I propped myself up, staring vacantly out the window. "No, I want to look him in the eye and tell him. Tell him I'm taking you out of here."

She bolted upright, glaring at me. "You're crazy. He'll kill the both of us. You're no match for him the shape you're in."

"That's what you think. I want to make sure it's over when we leave here. I don't want to slink off in the dark like a goddamn dog with its tail between its legs. I want to know if he's going to be after us, if we're going to have to look over our shoulders every day for the rest of our lives. He tries to stop us, I'll kill him, plain and simple."

"But Santo – "

"You can't change my mind, Lucy."

"But you don't know what he's like here. He's a high-powered character in Picayune. Just because he had regrets about shooting you up doesn't mean he won't do it again, this time for keeps. And even if he doesn't kill you, he'll probably get the sheriff to throw you in jail as soon as you turn your back. He'll have me out of here, and you won't be able to lift a finger because you'll be in the calaboose."

I gave her a cold, hard stare because I was feeling stubborn. I knew I had to do it my way or not do it at all. I didn't want to be second-guessing myself later.

She turned away from me to face the wall.

Soon I was asleep.

The next thing I knew it was morning. I could see through the cheap curtains that it was overcast outside. The gloomy, hidden sun wasn't very high up in the sky so I knew it still had to be early. Pulling on my raggedy, smelly clothes, it struck me that I'd better scrounge up something new. How I would pay for it was another story.

A few minutes later I was downstairs at the registration desk, the clerk giving me his cockeyed stare.

"Haven't seen Mr. Cameron or Miss Damien this morning?"

"Eh?" His eyes crossed, and I thought, hell, maybe they were registered under other names, too. I was sure Leroi was.

"Never mind."

I went into the saloon and wolfed down a big breakfast of bacon, eggs and hash browns. I was finishing my coffee with a piece of stale bread when Lucy came in and sat beside me.

"I'm glad you're here. I just came from your room and thought maybe you'd gotten mad and left."

I leaned over to buss her on the cheek. "You think I could possibly leave without you?"

She didn't smile or anything. Instead she got serious as hell.

"Santo, we've got to get out of here. As soon as possible. We should've left last night like I wanted."

"I told you. First, I want to tell Leroi I'm taking you out of here."

"Oh, you stupid idiot!" She jumped up, throwing her chair back so hard it toppled over. "You want to see him? Well? Come on then!" She grabbed my hand and tugged me away, making a beeline for the stairs. I threw coins on the table and let her drag me up to the second floor. It was all that I could do to keep up with her.

She didn't knock at that door at the end of the hall, Leroi's door. She dug beneath her petticoat, came up with a key, unlocked it, and we were inside the dingy room.

Leroi lay on the floor by the window, a breeze blowing his lanky hair across his face. His eyes had a look of complete disbelief. There was a bullet hole smack dab in the middle of his forehead.

"I shot him."

9

I caught myself staring at the bloody floor.

"When I told him we were running away together, he said he was going to go down and plug you while you were still asleep. Then he came after me with this." She tossed a long, straight knife, a dagger like knife-throwers in the circus use, at my feet. It clattered past Leroi's head. "I wanted to kill the bastard anyway, ever since I laid eyes on him."

Her gold wedding ring, the one she'd gotten when she took her vows at the convent in St. Louis, glinted in the light of the still burning bedside lamp, and I thought about just how far down she'd sunk. I didn't know whether to thank her for saving my life or thrash her within an inch of hers. I wondered if she was telling me the truth or elaborately embroidering what had happened.

"Now do you see? We've got to get out of here, out of Picayune before the sheriff and his other friends find out that he's dead."

I sat down on the red satin bedspread that covered the four-poster. Despite the unscrubbed walls, the late Leroi Cameron's room was considerably nicer than mine. Bigger, too. But then he had had the money to pay for it. To pay for the best.

Without another word, she picked up a valise from beside the bed, came over to me and opened it right under my nose. It was a bag full of five, ten, twenty and fifty dollar bills arranged in neat stacks.

"It's ours, Santo. We can go as far, get as far away as we want. We could go to China."

I knocked the bag out of her hand and the bills went scattering over Leroi. She scrambled to pick them up, getting down on all fours so she looked like a dog. It was so goddamn pathetic I started getting sick to my stomach.

"I don't want any part of that money, Lucy."

She turned around, still on her hands and knees, and looked at me like I was crazy.

"You goddamn hypocrite. Leroi told me about you. What you and he and those other sons-of-bitches did during the war. And you in penitentiary for however long you were in for."

"That's behind me now. I wouldn't touch that money because of the way Leroi got it. Those men on the train… he just lined them up and shot them. Executed them! You understand? Put them to death like he was God!"

She had gathered all the money and put it back inside the bag, then gotten up with it, a forlorn expression on her face. "Why do you think I killed him?"

"If we take that money we're as bad as him."

She shook her head, giving up on me. She knew I was right but didn't give a damn. Everything she'd been through had hardened her, changed her so that she was worse than me. I could tell by the way she held her shoulders so rigid, the way her fingers clutched and unclutched the grip of the valise that what I was talking about was something she wanted to forget. Her conscience was a millstone around her beautiful, delicate neck, and she wanted to be rid of it before it strangled her.

Setting the bag down on the floor beside the fireplace, she pulled out a stack of tens and one of twenties. She wrapped them up in a handkerchief, knotted the four corners together, and tossed the small bundle up on the bed beside me.

"We've got to have something to stake us till we get where we're going."

I gave her a blank stare. She turned back to the bag, but her eyes were on the smoking embers glowing on the hearth. Abruptly she upended the valise with both hands, emptying and shaking it back and forth till every bill lay in a heap on the red coals. They caught fire almost immediately, and she sat cross-legged on the floor, watching the small fortune flicker brightly in orange and yellow flames, going up in smoke.

Even though it made me feel like an idiot, I was glad she'd done it. It hadn't taken that much persuading to make her see that there was just no chance on earth that we could start out that way, living from and squandering blood money. I had my doubts about those bills she'd peeled off, but she was right, we couldn't head anywhere with absolutely nothing. Especially if some crooked sheriff and his cronies were going to jump on our trail the minute they knew Leroi was dead.

She swiveled around on her knees, grimaced as if to say "what the hell".

"Dannahy, the sheriff, already got a cut of $5,000. Leroi didn't tell him anywhere near how much there was. Maybe he won't be so quick to give us grief."

"It's Federal money. They would have posted it straight away. He knows. He'll think we're making off with the rest. He'll be on our ass so fast it'll make your head swim."

She gave me a dirty look. "Yeah, I suppose you're right about him coming after us. I'm not using my head," her look turned to ice, "not like you."

I let that go and stood up. "We'd better get out now, I don't reckon you've got much more to pack than the last time I saw you."

She reached in the closet, produced a suede coat that was two sizes too big for her, shrugged into it and opened the door for me with a self-satisfied smirk.

"There's a chill outside."

I pointed to the coat. "That's it?"

"That's it." She scooped the bundle of tens and twenties off the bed and pocketed it. "Looks like you were going to leave without. That's not very prudent, Mr. Brady."

I picked up Leroi's Winchester, then stopped next to her. "What're you going to do for a horse? We can't double up on mine. It'd cave in on us."

"We're not taking your horse. Leroi didn't keep his two mounts in the stable. He kept them tied up in the alley out back… in case he had to get out quick. Just like we've got to do right now."

I followed her down a back staircase to the rear. Luckily there wasn't anybody around. The two horses, a pinto and a small roan, stood idly outside. I boosted her onto the roan.

"Too bad we couldn't wait till dark."

She rolled her eyes. "Too bad Leroi was so set on killing you right then or we could have."

I grimaced. "Whatever you say, honey."

We steered the horses away from the hotel and down the alley. I let her lead since she seemed to know the layout. On the way, I happened to glance up at the back windows to Marleybone's office. They were coated with a thick layer of dust, but I could still make out his quizzical, unshaven face peering down at us.

"Marleybone a friend of Dannahy's?"

She twisted around, followed my gaze and made a disgusted face. "Not particularly. I don't like it, though, him seeing us sneaking off like this."

"Too late now."

"Yeah."

10

We didn't take the main roads, but dirt paths through the woods that skirt Lake Pontchartrain. It was the long way around, but the safest. Right before we got to Louisiana, I swung a long, wide willow branch behind us, letting it drag on the trail to mess up our tracks. After a mile or so of that, we switched over to following a shallow stream.

Lucy wasn't any stranger to riding, and it was really something to watch, the way she handled a horse. By that time not much about her could surprise me. I was ready for just about anything. One thing I could tell, she truly did love me. Her burning up the money, letting that much cold hard cash go up in flames was all the proof anyone could need.

Once or twice while we were splashing along that creek, she'd nudge her mount close to me, then smile and pat my hand.

"Santo, I feel so good right now. I'm so happy we found each other again. I've never felt this free before, not in my whole sorry life."

She bent over and kissed me on the cheek. I reined back on the horse, put my lips to hers, and we sat there kissing. That and the gurgling of the brook were the only sounds. Suddenly the breeze became stronger and colder, putting a chill in the air that made the both of us tremble. Shocked to alertness, I thought of Dannahy and pulled away from her.

"We'd better get going. Once our friend Dannahy finds Leroi, he's not going to just let it lie. Believe me."

It was something she didn't want to think about. She became sullen, pursing her lips in a pouty sneer and kicking her horse so it trotted away from me. She turned back, giving me a cold hard stare.

"Don't you worry, Santo Brady. We can take care of that bastard Dannahy, and any artillery he throws at us."

I shrugged and caught up with her.

"I'm not worried about Dannahy alone. But it won't be just Dannahy alone. It'll be a whole posse."

She didn't want to be bothered by what she figured were insignificant details.

"You know we aren't just one gun." She pulled a Peacemaker out of the grimy suede coat and clasped it in her dainty hand like she knew how to handle it. "We're two. You haven't seen me shoot yet. I'll give you a run for your money."

I didn't doubt her and smiled. "Okay, honey. You've been calling the shots on the mark so far."

That didn't satisfy her. "Sure you're not waiting for me to fall flat on my face?"

I shook my head. "What do you think?"

She blushed, her cheeks turning a hot red. "I'm sorry. For some reason I'm not thinking straight."

We spurred the horses and cut through the stream at a healthy trot. We didn't see a soul till we hit the outskirts of New Orleans. The creek current had become too deep, too strong, because of the Mississippi feeding into her. So, instead of coming through the water, we shuffled along the banks. Dirt poor Negro sharecroppers and their shanties dotted the shore, growing in number the closer we came to the city. Gradually the air became thick with the smell of primitive Creole cooking and the musical patois of the people.

Except for the children, no one paid any attention to us. It must've been Lucy's red dress, looking for all the world like a patch of flame, that attracted them. Her horse's gentle shifting back and forth created a languid spell, making her look like the centerpiece on some giant music box, and the effect on the kids was hypnotic.

"Hey, mister! Hey, missy! We hungry!"

Their skinny, undernourished hands reached up to us, palms open, grasping for the money we could give them – for anything we could give them. Neither of us had any coins. It was probably just as well. Giving them a little would be worse than giving them nothing at all. And handing them one of our stolen bills would have been suicide. What and how much they needed we could never give them anyway. It didn't stop them. Except for an occasional scolding by some watchful parent, they ran after us, the already dirty rags they wore splattered by the mud of the rutted path along the embankment. They kept up with us until we reached the main road, then suddenly lost interest.

Lucy turned to look after them. "Poor little things. They remind me of the children I used to see outside the convent walls back in St. Louis." She shifted, holding up her head to watch the cloudy sky and then the metropolis that lay ahead. I knew that there was a stormy conflict brewing inside of her, and I was at a loss on how to put her at ease.

"I used to wonder every waking moment why God let poor little ones starve, be beaten by cruel parents and left finally to die in the gutters of cold, uncaring cities. It bothered me. It still bothers me."

"There's not much you can do about it."

"No. I understand now. I really do. That's the hard side of God. If there wasn't such a horror and hardship and suffering, there wouldn't be anything to fight against. Life wouldn't have any joys, either. So we do the best we can spitting in the face of monsters."

We kept on that way for another couple of hours. We didn't stop until we reached the far side of the city, a ramshackle hotel on the southwestern tip. A hundred years before it may have been a sterling example of French architecture, but now it was a sorry mess. What had once been delicate iron latticework down the center of its front had turned into a tangle of green corrosion. The walls on either side of the second and third story windows bore savage-looking marks in the masonry where the balconies had been torn free.

"This is appropriate." The spires of an ancient Catholic church loomed against the cloud-hidden sun directly across the street. "I can go to Mass in the morning."

"Tomorrow's Sunday?"

She shook her head, amused at my puzzlement. "You don't know what day it is, do you?"

"I just realized it. I haven't had too much time to give it any thought."

"Well, tonight's Saturday night. A night to celebrate our new-found freedom. A night to celebrate that we're together and both still alive." She laughed cynically, pressing herself against me as I slipped off my horse, then kissing me wetly on the mouth. "What do you say we go in and have a drink?"

I smiled as she took my hand. We tied the horses to a hitching post, then, holding each other tight, waltzed into the hotel's darkened, rundown lobby.

I hadn't realized it outside, but it was a Negro hotel, and I turned to leave. Lucy planted her feet steadfastly before the registration desk, holding onto my arm and refusing to budge.

"We're staying here, Santo. It's the safest place."

It really didn't matter, I suppose, but I figured that the hotel probably wouldn't want any part of us. I was ready to agree with her but was stopped by a gigantic black woman who walked out from behind a bead-shrouded doorway and propped herself up on the less-than-substantial countertop.

"It may be the safest place, young lady, for whatever reason, but you an' you acquaintance are sure as blazes not no way goin' to stay here. Am I understood?"

"You think I'm white, don't you?" Lucy drew a finger across her forehead. "I ain't but a third white. I'm one part colored, one part Blackfoot, too. And this here gentleman of mine and I are willing to pay good money to stay here."

"You a crazy bitch." The fat, charcoal-colored woman raised her eyebrows. "How much money you got, honeychile?"

Lucy pulled out a twenty and set it down on the desk. "That's for a week's stay with meals and whiskey."

The woman hesitated, and Lucy casually threw down another twenty. It was obviously more money than the proprietress had seen in quite some time. She snatched it up and tucked it out of sight in her ample cleavage.

"Come wit' me."

"Excuse me, ma'am."

She turned and looked defiantly in my face. "Yeah?"

"Aren't you forgetting something?"

"Now what might that be?"

"Don't you want us to sign the register?"

"Honey, money like that and the ways you two be lookin' together, hell, I was sure you rather not sign no name to nothin'."

She was right, and I smiled. She gave me a funny look and shook her head, then led the way to a staircase with no banisters. We didn't turn off at the second floor but kept climbing up the creaking, worm-eaten steps to a third story. A few boarders who looked like regulars – an old man with no teeth, two whores, one Indian and one black, both loaded down with gaudy paste jewelry – gave us the once over as the huge proprietress steered us down the shadowy hall to the very last room on the floor. The atmosphere was stale and oppressive, and it smelled like the other tenants had been cooking in their rooms. It was surprising that the building hadn't turned to ashes long ago.

"This is it. Here's the key. I'll send up a bottle of whiskey in a few minutes."

She started to leave, but Lucy caught up with her.

"The money for the whiskey is meant for good liquor, not grain alcohol with weak tea added in for color."

"You don' have insult me, missy. It be good stuff. Sealed, too."

"Thanks."

Her eyes were smoldering coals as she turned in a huff and headed back down the stairs. The old man and the whores stood outside their open doors gawking at us until Lucy took hold of my arm and pulled me inside the room.

It was dingy, sparsely put together, the sole piece of furniture consisting of a narrow double bed equipped with a spotted mattress and no bedclothes. An old burlap potato sack hung across the window as curtain.

I gingerly touched the mattress.

"We better turn this sucker over or else we're going to get bitten by all the bedbugs in New Orleans."

She grabbed one end, I took the other, and we flipped it. An age-old bloodstain in the shape of a giant, warped four leaf clover graced the other side. She smiled up at me. "I never did see two luckier people." She fell up against me. "Don't you worry about anything, Santo. You stay here and rest. I'm going to go out to buy sheets and a blanket. *Clean* sheets and a blanket." She stopped, glancing around the room to see what else was needed to supply us with bare essentials. Spotting the remains of a melted candle that had burnt a hole in the floor on one side of the bed, she added, "And an oil lamp."

"Don't spend too much. We're not going to be able to take every single little thing with us when we leave."

"I'm not thinking about that. I'm thinking about making us comfortable. About making you comfortable. You're still not all back in one piece." She gently pushed me down on the bed. "You're still not healed up, honey. I'm going to change and clean those dressings when I get back." She kissed me on the forehead and cheek. "Okay?"

I smiled.

"Are you going to relax now?"

I nodded. "Yeah."

She opened the window for me, checked the bundle of money, burying it deep in the pocket of her suede coat, blew me a kiss and left.

I sank back onto the dirty mattress, so tired I didn't give a damn if the last occupant had had TB, the bubonic plague or been shot to death on the very spot. I fell asleep almost immediately, slipping into a dreamless slumber that lasted until Lucy returned.

It had gotten considerably darker while I'd slept. She hadn't made a sound when she'd come back in – I'd simply woken up with the feeling somebody was in the room – and I had to strain to make out her silhouette against the window. She was crouched on the floor, holding the burlap curtain so only a sliver of grayness came through. She seemed agitated; studying whatever was going on in the street below.

"What's the matter? Why so jumpy?"

She didn't answer, instead uncorking the whiskey bottle that had come while I was asleep. She belted down a sizable swig then threw it to me without looking up. Even though I caught it, some of it splashed out on me and the bundles she'd brought in.

"Hey, easy. No point in wasting good liquor."

Once again she didn't reply, just kept staring out the window.

I gulped down at least two shots. "So you saw something while you were out?"

She slowly turned her head. "Not something. Someone. Several 'someones'. Several 'someones' whom I prayed to God I'd never see again in my whole life."

"Who?"

"Well, for one, Dannahy. And Marleybone, that two-faced son-of-a-bitch. And a couple of ugly bastards I've never seen before. Probably deputies. But that isn't the worst of it."

"Yeah?"

"Yeah. My father and my brother Charlie were with them."

11

Needless to say the news served to pretty much ruin our evening. Lucy had been all for hightailing it immediately, running out on the situation as fast as we could. But I'd managed to convince her that the best thing to do would be staying put for at least a day or two until we could tell just how hot we really were. I knew that Dannahy had been bound to come into New Orleans anyway. It was only how quick he'd managed it that had us spooked. I knew the posse picking up our actual trail was impossible. I'd been too exacting in covering our tracks. Marleybone, though, had seen us leaving Picayune in a southwesterly direction and had undoubtedly tipped off Dannahy and his deputies as quickly as he could hobble across the street. As far as Lucy's father and brother having hooked up with them, well, it was anybody's guess.

Lucy hadn't wanted to leave her place by the window, but I'd finally succeeded in coaxing her to bed at what must've been about ten o'clock. The proprietress had brought us a meal of cornbread, salty black beans, rice and weak chicory. We lay there with the new brass oil lamp Lucy'd bought burning low, dawdling over the food, eating in silence. Or should I say I ate mine. Lucy glared at the grimy wall, scarcely touching her plate.

"C'mon, honey, you've got to eat. You've got to keep up your strength."

She ignored me, picking up the tray from her lap and setting it on the floor

"I can't figure how the hell this sheriff Dannahy met up with your father and brother."

She continued gazing off into space but reached into the pocket of the suede coat, pulling forth two crumpled envelopes. The one that was torn along one edge she handed to me.

"I found that in the coat while I was out buying things."

I pulled a creased, well-thumbed handbill from the envelope and unfolded it. Two daguerreotype likenesses of Lucy stared up at me. One showed her in her religious garb, her habit I think they call it, from when she was a novice at the convent. The other picture was a shocking contrast, Lucy clad in a bawdy dancehall dress with a gravely downtrodden look on her pretty, wild-eyed face. The legend: MISSING – LUCILLE ONEONTA DAMIEN OF ST. LOUIS, MISSOURI was emblazoned across the top of the paper. Below was a detailed description of her, including her father's opinion that she had been kidnapped by gypsies and sold to a white slaver. Below that, in extremely large red letters was: REWARD FOR INFORMATION LEADING TO HER DISCOVERY – $10,000.

"Leroi recognized me the minute he laid his eyes on me back at the train. That's why he dragged me off." She handed me the other envelope. "I found this, too. It made sense out of something that Leroi said to me just before I shot him."

I opened the second envelope, which was actually addressed to Leroi care of the hotel in Picayune. A formal letter from a physician named Douglas at the St. James Hospital in New Orleans, it explained to a Mr. Leroi Enoch Cameron that he was in the terminal stages of tuberculosis and it was better than even money he wouldn't make it through the next two months. The letter was dated three weeks previous. I let it fall on the floor, sank back on the bed and sighed.

"What did he say that you understand now?"

"When he found out I was going to leave him, he laughed, a strange sick laugh wracked with coughing. And he seemed so pathetic, so sad, I felt sorry for him... until he picked up the knife." She swigged a good healthy dose of the whiskey. "He stood up very deliberately and started towards me. He said he'd rather spend one good week with me, then die, than ever give me up to you. I suddenly realized how right you were about him being in love with me. But I didn't know how much else there was to it, that he really didn't have anything to lose.

"The way he looked at me, I knew he meant business. But I told him I was still going. When I pointed the gun at him, he smiled and said that I'd be doing him a favor if that's the way I truly felt about him. He jumped at me, and I pulled the trigger."

She clasped her hands together and brought them to her face in a fit of guilty anguish.

"He was one of the only close friends I had during the war. It's hard to believe."

She shook her head. "He felt bad about leaving you to die. Then again, just before I shot him, he was determined to blast you from the face of the earth. There was something inside him, something rock-hard that had taken over. Something dead and smothering and ruthless that had suffocated his heart until any true feeling was buried…"

She reached for the whiskey.

"The poor bastard. I know both his brother and father died in Yankee prison camps. His mother, wife and sister were all killed at Vicksburg. After the war was over, he had nobody. Tell me something, Lucy…"

All of a sudden she looked at me like she remembered what I was to her, and I could see it kind of startled her. She sank down on the bed, her legs till hanging off onto the floor and her head and shoulders cradled in the crook of my arm. She nestled closer.

"What?"

"Why are your father and brother so set on finding you? Why do they give a good goddamn if you want to take off and live your own life, make your own decisions?"

"Because that's not the kind of people they are. My father's changed over the last ten years from a fair-minded, life-loving person to a twisted phony, scared of his own shadow, obsessed with proving himself, with following every bullheaded impulse he has to stick to his 'principles.' His kindness and philanthropic endeavors during the last couple of years have been a sham, a shallow excuse, a good habit he can't shake.

"Mama dying was the last straw. She became sick and it took her several years to die. He blamed her for it – I could tell – her and her Blackfoot ancestry for deserting him. Even though I didn't see him after she died, I could tell from Charlie that Papa felt betrayed, like it was her personal, Indian brand of vengeance on the white man."

I gave her a weird look.

"Yeah," she laughed, "he's not a particularly straight-thinking fellow. And with Charlie in tow egging him on, well, you can see why all this is happening. That I turned my back on a religious vocation, left the convent – it was an insidious evil to him. And it was all the worse because God, Jesus, my husband supposedly got stabbed in the back by me, his daughter, his kith and kin."

She laughed again, and I could see that she was pretty drunk.

"But you know, if Jesus really does care, I know he's not ticked off at me. He knows that I still love Him even though we're not together anymore."

She said it as a joke, comparing Jesus to an earthly spouse she'd jilted and done wrong to, but I saw the glistening tears in her eyes and knew it wasn't far from the truth. She sat up, giving me a concerned look.

"I'm sorry, Santo. I completely forgot about changing your bandages."

"It's okay. We've got all the time in the world."

It wasn't till she pulled away the dressing on my shoulder that the wound started to throb, sending waves of pulsing heat up my neck into my head. I glanced over as she peeled away the dirty cloth and almost fainted. The hole was an ugly combination of blackened, coagulated blood and orange-ish flesh. Lucy winced but didn't say anything, just moved over to my side wound, then the one on my hand. Both of them looked in better condition.

"I don't like the way your shoulder looks, Santo. It might be infected. I'm surprised you don't have a fever."

The sight of the open, garish-colored wound quickened my pulse and sent anxious shivers down my spine. I'd seen a few men die a prolonged, agonizing death from gangrene during the war, and I was damned if I was going to end up in the same boat.

"Tell you what... that huge lady we're paying so well to be our benefactor looks like she might know some home cures that'll be just what the doctor ordered."

"Whatever you do, don't tell her it's for bullet wounds. She'd use it as a gun to our head at the drop of a hat."

"Don't worry, I'll tell her you're a matador with an old bull-fighting injury."

I laughed, and it hurt to laugh.

"I'll be back before you know it." Then she was gone. I stared up at the dingy ceiling with its unpainted, rotting timbers and listened to the click-clack of her heels going down the hall, then down the stairs into the depths of the building. I fell into a restless half-sleep until she returned.

When she came back she had a large, bulky muslin bag and several folded pieces of white cotton in her hands.

"It only cost me a dollar, and I watched her while she made it up nice and fresh. So now I have exactly what you need." She pulled out a glass jar of foul-smelling black paste, then a smaller vial of clear liquid. Somehow the words, "nice and fresh" didn't seem to apply. "If this poultice doesn't do the trick nothing will. That gal sure does know her home remedies." She uncorked the vial of clear liquid.

"What's that?"

She held up the paste. "She swore me to secrecy about this…" Then, smirking, she wearily shook her head at my anxiety. "The watery stuff is a mixture of herbs and diluted snake venom. To clean it out." She tried to keep from laughing as my eyes widened. "Don't worry, it's not that strong. I have to put it on first to prepare for the poultice."

The clear, crystalline drops stung like hell and immediately numbed the surrounding tissue. It also sent me into a hallucinatory delirium that, even now, I can barely recall. It seemed there were several other people in the room besides Lucy. And everyone of them was dead – my mother, Millie, Leroi – all hovering in the shadows around the bed.

The poultice was a boiling mess against my skin. I felt it drip down through the bullet hole, blistering and purifying each festering inch of pus-lined flesh.

She ended by tearing long strips of white cotton, then winding them under my arm and over the top of my shoulder. She did the same on my hand and side. When she was completely done, she lingered for a few minutes at the window, lackadaisically sipping the whiskey and eyeballing the thoroughfare in front of the hotel.

At last she crawled into bed beside me and, without a word, fell fast asleep.

12

Sometime in the small hours of the morning I woke to find her pacing the floor beside the window. I knew she was really worked up about what was going to happen next. I propped myself on my good arm, and she glanced over at me. My fever had broken, and I was the most clearheaded I'd been in several hours.

"I've been thinking…" She sat down on the edge of the bed, but turned away, afraid to look me in the eye. "I've been thinking you'd have a better chance, we'd both have a better chance of making it if we split up. You know, meet some place later, say in a couple of weeks."

I shook my head. "I don't think so. I think we'd both have less of a chance. If we stay together –" She gave me an exasperated look but let me continue. " – Lucy, I know we can both take care of ourselves. We should stick together. That way both of us – "

She cut me off. "Yeah, I've seen us both in action. Like back at the train. We sure handled ourselves swell back there."

I felt my cheeks flush, and I glared at her. Seeing her give off such a defiant iciness made me angry. "Lucy, we're not splitting up. That's final. The best thing for us to do would be to go down to the levee at dawn and book passage up the Mississippi as far as we can go. Just get the hell out of here before they can catch up to us."

"Doing something like that'd leave a hell of a trail, now, wouldn't it. We might as well put signposts up where we're headed. Better yet, why don't we send them a letter and a map where we are right now. Hell, let's make it as easy as we can for them."

I didn't say anything more, just lay back down and stared at the ceiling. She was probably right. She reached out for my good hand and squeezed it with an iron grip.

"I'm sorry, Santo. This isn't your fault. None of it's your fault. I'm feeling backed into a corner, that's all. Either I stay in the frying pan or jump in the goddamn fire. There's no way out. Thinking about it is driving me crazy."

"Well, don't think about it. We'll get out of this. There's no reason why we shouldn't... if we use our heads and reason things out. And don't panic."

She came back to bed and lay down beside me. If I hadn't felt that I knew her so well, I wouldn've sworn she was suddenly bashful of me. Why, I don't know. She wrapped her arms around my chest, slowly raised herself and kissed the bandage covering my shoulder.

"How's that feeling?"

"A lot better, thanks to you."

"You'll be okay as long as we keep it clean while it's healing."

"Yeah."

Then she changed the subject back to how we were going to get out of the mess.

"You truly think the steamboat north is our best way out?"

I nodded.

"Well, if we're going to do it, I do want to do it in the morning. And I want to be down there at the levee before dawn."

"We should both get some sleep then. We're going to need it."

She batted her eyes, flirting with me. "I don't think I can sleep."

"Well, honey, what'll help you get to sleep?"

She smiled and kissed me on the cheek. I moved my mouth up to hers, and we kissed. And kept on kissing while she slipped off the rest of her clothes.

13

It was still pitch black outside when we left the hotel. One lone street lamp flickered in front of the church across the way. We carefully negotiated the muddy walk to the shabby livery stable next door.

"Santo, I can't see a goddamn thing."

"Just hold onto my coat and stay right beside me. If we want to make sure no one sees us, we can't even light a match."

The stable door creaked on its rusty hinges as we eased it open. But when we finally stood before the stalls where both of our horses should've been, we found them empty.

"Christ! I knew we couldn't trust that fat bitch. She knew we were in trouble and wouldn't dare squawk to the law about something like this."

"Well, we'll just have to walk."

I gave her a questioning look. "How close are we to the levee?"

"I'm not sure. It might be as much as a couple of miles."

"To hell with that. Turnabout's fair play." I grabbed the reins of the only two decent-looking nags in the place and pulled them out.

"Santo, you know what'll happen if we get caught?"

"Yeah, yeah, I know. They'll drag us to the nearest oak and string us up."

She didn't say anything else but inched the door open to see how safe the street looked.

"Okay."

I was on my horse by then. Lucy mounted hers, and we cantered out into the open. Once we had the doors closed, we trotted down the street about a block, then broke into a gallop. Lucy knew the way more or less so it only took about fifteen minutes. We abandoned the horses two blocks from the levee and walked the rest of the way.

So as not to arouse suspicion, we decided to buy our tickets and board separately. The ticket office was already open, and Negro and Indian workers were loading copious amounts of freight onto the boat by way of a narrow, insubstantial gangplank.

The emaciated ticket agent scribbled furiously on a long, yellow sheet of paper beneath the meager light of a tiny oil lamp. I watched him working his gaunt face – his sunken cheeks, non-existent jaw, spectacles perched precariously on a hawk-nose – for nearly a minute before he raised his head and noticed me.

"One for St. Paul."

"Doesn't go that far. Not this boat anyway."

"Well, how far does it go?"

"St. Louis."

I frowned. That was one place we certainly had no desire to visit.

"How about Moline?"

"Yes."

"All right then."

He impatiently wrote out the ticket, took my money, then handed it to me.

"Be on the dock no later than 6:30. She'll leave about 7:30."

"Thanks." I started to leave but stopped when he called out after me.

"Any baggage, sir?"

"No."

He regarded me strangely, shrugged, then returned to his scribbling.

I rounded the corner of the alley where Lucy was waiting.

"I bought a ticket to Moline. But you buy one to St. Louis – "

She gave me a startled look.

"Let me finish. You don't get off there. You get off with me in Moline."

She understood and slowly nodded. "Okay. You scared me for a second." She made to leave to go buy her ticket, but I reached out and grabbed her.

"Let's wait ten minutes or so before you head over. It should be almost light by then."

I sat down with her on the narrow stairs leading up into grey shadows.

"You feeling better now?" I put my arm protectively around her. She looked so sweet and pretty sitting all bundled in that filthy suede coat.

"Yeah, I'm sorry I acted the way I did at the hotel." Abruptly, she rushed her mouth up to meet mine, and we sat kissing for quite a few minutes.

A tin can falling somewhere behind us made us both jump. We turned to see a huge black cat scurrying into a hole in the wall. Lucy was superstitious, and I could tell by the expression on her trembling face that the sight had disturbed her.

"You'd better go buy your ticket."

She snapped out of it, smiled and stood. "To hell with bad omens." I smiled back and watched her disappear around the corner. Grey light was flooding the alley, and I figured it must've been a little after six.

In a few minutes she was back.

"Any problems?"

"No."

We waited a little longer until we heard sounds of people congregating on the dock. She got real stubborn then and demanded that I be the first one to board, not her. I told her I'd flip her a coin, but she wouldn't go for it. I wanted to see her in comparative safety first, but she beat me to the punch and turned the whole thing around.

"Santo, it's going to cut my worries about a hundred percent if I see you getting onto that boat before me. I'll wait about thirty minutes, then I'll come on board, too."

"Well, we can't stand around here arguing all day." I gave her one last, hard peck on the cheek, then headed towards the dock.

The levee was already alive with people. I'd been wrong about the time. It was still pretty early, not quite half-past six, but the heat and humidity was already a palpable, living thing.

I pushed through the crowd to the gangplank and waited in the short line. A bunch of Shawnees and Seminoles were wrangling with each other about something a few yards to my left, and I wondered what both tribes were doing in that neck of the woods. They were hawking trinkets – jewelry, furs, blankets – to travelers from up north and competing for a limited number of customers. It was a friendly kind of rivalry, though, and I smiled because they were obviously having fun with each other.

Then I was on board. A steward showed me to my cabin, and, as soon as I took a gander at it, I headed up to the top deck to watch for Lucy.

I didn't worry at first because I figured she wanted to take her time, be careful coming out into the open, into the crowd. But when the thirty minutes were up, when it was going on an hour, and they were going to be pulling in the gangplank to cast off, I have to admit I started to worry. I tried looking out over the city, enjoying the delicate lines of eighteenth century architecture, then looking north to where the trees and swampland branched off the river.

It was a clear day, no clouds in the sky, and the sun was getting to me. I felt there was something wrong, but it wasn't anything I could put my finger on. There hadn't been any commotion down on the dock. And I hadn't seen hide nor hair of anybody resembling her father or brother, or Dannahy's posse.

Suddenly the boat shot off its whistle and I jumped. I knew all at once that something had happened, and she wasn't coming. Either she couldn't come because they'd found her, or else she'd decided to run out on me. Both ideas didn't make any sense, though, and I kept on trying to figure it, hoping against hope that she'd suddenly appear down below. I was turning around, my eyes still fixed on the dock, when a heavy tread fell behind me.

A balled-up fist glanced off my ear as I feinted to the right against the rotten wood railing. Whoever he was, he knew what he was doing because the momentum of the blow didn't plunge him forward over and down to the dock. Instead he braced himself, blocking my knee as I brought it up into his groin. I got away from the railing fast, but a small, wiry, baby-faced kid came from behind him, boxing me in. I bent over double and charged, butting my head into the kid's stomach. He puked as I whirled to get out of his way, and I just missed getting splattered by his breakfast. He started to cry, holding the railing with one hand and his stomach with the other. The bigger man stared at him like he was a bug he was going to squash, then looked at me the same way. He was a good head taller than me with a mass of thick black hair and the broadest set of shoulders I'd ever seen. Except for the cruel black snake eyes, I immediately saw the family resemblance and knew

I was up against Charlie, Lucy's brother. He started for me with a slow deliberate walk that sent a chill up my spine. His hands were the size of my head, and he had a reach on him that wouldn't put any self-respecting gorilla to shame.

I backed up as quickly as I could, but the narrow deck afforded me scant room to maneuver. I fumbled for my gun, but he lunged at me so fast it fell out of its holster and through the railing, splashing into the Mississippi. I went over backwards into some old lady with a parasol, and giant Charlie crashed down on the both of us. She let out with the most godawful shriek you ever heard. It had a strange effect on Charlie because he shifted his weigh a bit while he pummeled my face, and I got the idea he was actually concerned about her. I tried the knee trick again, and it worked, doubling him over and making his fists reflex away from the vicinity of my face to his own privates. Blood was in my eyes, but I could see that he was incapacitated for a few seconds. I felt around for the lady's parasol, found it, aimed it like a pool cure, and shot him with its pointed end right between the eyes. That toppled him backwards and off of me.

I scrambled to my feet, climbing behind the old lady who was already being helped by an elderly Negro porter. The whole boat was up in arms what with all the commotion, and I was expecting trouble from the bottom deck any second.

Charlie was coming back to his senses. Meanwhile, I'd lost track of the kid that had been with him.

"You little bastard!" I could tell by his tone of voice that there wasn't any love lost between us. "I'm going to enjoy this!"

Whatever he meant, I wasn't going to hang around to find out. I ran along the deck to the opposite end of the boat. The one time I snuck a glance over my shoulder I saw Charlie on his feet coming towards me again with his slow, steady gait. Suddenly six angry, burly men appeared behind him. I prayed my salvation was at hand. But hope was nipped in the bud. Charlie pulled aside his coat lapels to show them the tin star pinned to his vest.

I knew I was sunk but kept on running. Just before I made it to the end where the deck looped and jutted out a few feet over the giant paddle, the lank-haired kid whirled around the corner, a Remington Army pistol in his fist. He had a badge on, too, and sure seemed to be enjoying the power he thought it gave him. Behind me, the mob was closing in. Yeah, I reckoned the jig was really up when suddenly the whistle blasted again, the paddle began to turn, and the whole boat jolted forwards. Right against the railing, the kid lost his balance, lurching back and over. The gun went off once as he fell headfirst into the rotating blades.

I was about to shinny over the rail and down one of the support poles to the bottom deck when something dull and heavy banged into the base of my neck, and everything went black.

14

I awoke to find myself staring at a pearly white ceiling. A cold breeze chilled me to the bone. I tried to sit up but couldn't manage it; it hurt too much. My ribs felt cracked, if not completely busted, and there was the sour taste of old blood in my mouth.

"Charles, our guest is awake." It was an old man's voice, quavery yet filled with a nervous energy.

Shadows of the men in the room cast by the late afternoon sun loomed menacingly against alabaster walls. The noise of a teeming marketplace welled-up from the street below and echoed in the vaulted emptiness of the chamber.

With a lot of difficulty, I propped myself on both elbows. The old man was in a high-backed wicker throne slightly to the left of the open French windows. Beside the old man was a small table and chair where Marleybone had parked himself, tippling a water-glass full of whiskey and playing solitaire. The man I took to be Dannahy stood with his back to everyone, gazing stonily out the window. Charlie sat cross-legged on the floor on the other side of his father.

"My poor boy, what happened to your face?" The old man's attempt at sarcasm made me sick to my stomach.

"I cut myself shaving."

Marleybone harrumphed, suppressing laughter.

The old man continued. "Mr. Brady, I'm genuinely hurt that you've taken this tack with us. We are all, every one of us here, gentlemen and therefore abhor resorting to violence. It is a crude, animalistic way of communicating best left to forms of life lower on God's totem pole."

"I take it you haven't seen your sonny boy in action lately."

He ignored the jibe, but Charlie's eyes nailed me to the spot.

"Mr. Brady, I desire to know the whereabouts of my daughter. Immediately. The longer we waste time here with you, the less likely we are to find her."

Charlie looked up respectfully at the old man. "We'll find her, Pa."

The old man smiled. "Mr. Brady, my name is Edward Damien. Does that name mean anything to you?"

I shook my head.

"Well, it should. I am one of the wealthiest men west of the Mississippi. I have the power to impart an ungodly sum to you for information on the whereabouts of my daughter, Lucille, who, until recently, was in your company."

Dannahy turned around at that, frustration and resentment etched deeply in his taut, leathery face. "Whoa there, Mr. Damien. I was the one who found her. I was the one who wired you. That reward is mine."

The old man leaned forwards and defiantly jutted out his chin. "Leroi Cameron was the one who wired me about Lucille, not you, Dannahy. And Mr. Cameron is no longer with us."

Dannahy divided his stare between the both of us, looking for all the world like he was going to pop a blood vessel. A thick, ropy vein stood out on his forehead, and I half-expected it to burst, showering the milky white tile floor with blood.

The old man sank back into a more relaxed position. "Of course, Sheriff, you'll see a goodly portion of the reward money for your invaluable assistance in tracking Lucille and Mr. Brady."

Charlie gave a disgusted smirk. "Yeah, invaluable."

Marleybone laughed, and Dannahy went red as a beet, puffing himself up then storming out of the room.

"We're wasting precious time, Mr. Brady."

I sat up straight to get a better look at the old man and winced from the stabbing sensation in my chest.

"We are waiting, Mr. Brady. Things could be decidedly unpleasant for you if you continue along this course."

"You're getting mad, aren't you, old man? So what? I don't give a damn. I'm not telling you anything."

The old man's face didn't betray any big change in sentiment, but he nodded gravely at Charlie.

Charlie, all six and a half feet of him, was suddenly towering over me. Without a word of warning he stepped onto my bandaged hand, grinding in his boot heel with all of his weight behind it, and I screamed.

The fire springing from my hand along the veins and nerves and welling into my head shut out everything else. I couldn't hear their voices or see their faces, everything that existed had centralized itself into the hammering of my heart.

And through that white hot poker of pain, as he continued to stand on my now bleeding hand, I thought about what the hell I was doing. My life was a worthless mess, a slag heap of despair and horror anesthetized with drink until I'd met Lucy. She wasn't my salvation by a long shot. That's not what I was thinking. But for all her shortcomings and faults, she still gave me something. I don't think I'd realized how bankrupt my life was until I'd met her. She was a lot like me in so many ways. And knowing and being with her had shown me another way to live besides the day-to-day ritual of muddle-headed drifting. It made me feel that maybe together we could change things for ourselves, while apart we would flounder without meaning, without direction.

Then Charlie gave out what sounded like a Pawnee war-whoop, jumped into the air and came down squarely on my knuckles with both heels. I cried and shuddered. Bones cracked loudly, echoing in the room. Marleybone shivered in horror in spite of himself. Charlie walked over and leaned against the old man's chair.

"He isn't any good to us, Pa."

The old man frowned. "It'll be on your head, Mr. Brady, if Lucille comes to any harm before we reach her." He rose, sniffed, hypocritically crossed himself with a reverent, self-satisfied air, then tottered shakily in Marleybone's direction. In a sudden fit of anger he swept the table of cards and bottle. "Dress his wounds, my good quack, Marleybone. Perhaps you could actually perform some service for me, and I wouldn't feel that I was throwing my money away quite so flagrantly."

Marleybone dove for the whiskey glass, picking up the broken bottom half that still held an ounce or two. The old man shook his head in disgust, then exited the room. Charlie sauntered lazily over and kicked me in the face.

When I came to, Marleybone was hunched above me, his stale whiskey breath fouling the air and making me sick to my stomach. There was the fresh taste of blood in my mouth. I'd bitten off a tiny piece of the end of my tongue, and a broken front tooth clanked against its still firmly rooted brothers. Marleybone saw that I was awake and moved away from the red pulpy mess that was my hand. It felt dead from my wrist down.

"I'm sorry about all this, young fellow. If I had my way things would be handled quite a bit differently."

I spit the tooth and a wad of congealed blood in his face. He recoiled, wiping the stuff away with an already soiled coat sleeve.

"That's all right, Mr. Brady. I understand your feelings." He looked back down at my hand. "I'm afraid what with the bullet wound and then Charles' unsympathetic attitude about stepping on people, your hand won't be any good to you hence forward."

I sank my head back down on the cool tile floor.

"In fact, it's very likely what with the condition it's now in that you and your hand will soon have to part company."

I didn't believe him. I didn't want to. I told myself that he was just trying to scare me, get even with me for spitting in his face. It was going to take a hell of a struggle to get me to ever give up my hand. And no drunken, bounty-hungry quack was going to chop it off.

"Where am I?"

He answered without looking up from my hand. "The St. Lucy hotel."

He saw my derisive expression.

"No, really, that's its name. Honest to God. Old man Damien picked it for the obvious reason. You are sequestered in one of the larger suites." He continued bandaging and setting splints on the limp, swollen fingers. "Mr. Brady, I guarantee you your silence won't get you anywhere. Why don't you tell me? Where is your lady friend?"

I closed my eyes. I was as much in the dark as they were. Who knew where she was? She'd been smart to play it like she did. She'd been right, and I'd been all wrong. Hopefully she was safe wherever she was.

I passed out again.

15

When I came to, Marleybone was gone, and the room was in shadows.
I could tell the sun had already set. Somewhere behind me a door
closed, and what had been whispered voices rose up to a normal level.

"Why are you giving me all this grief, Charlie?"

"Mr. Damien to you, Dannahy. Because I don't like you. I don't
like anything about you. You're the worst kind of man. If you can even
call yourself a man. Look at you!"

I tried to turn my head. I could barely see their silhouettes
against the large double doors. Charlie grabbed hold of Dannahy's
rough, gangly hands.

"Look at your hands. A goddamn farmer who left his wife
and family to become a goddamn bounty hunter. And a goddamn poor
bounty hunter at that." His tone turned even nastier. "Playacting as a
sheriff." His cruel, piercing laugh was the icing on the cake.

"You've got no right to speak to me that way, Damien!" His
angry voice went up nearly an octave till it finally cracked with
suppressed fury. "The people of Picayune elected me fair and square.
I am a duly elected public official, and I'm doing my damnedest to
discharge my official duties."

"You pathetic tramp. The only person you've got convinced of
that is yourself. Come off it. You won't find that gullible rabble here."

"I'm telling you, Damien, you're going to push me too far.

My deputies are out after your whore sister right now. And when
they find her I've got a good mind to arrest her and take her back to
Picayune to stand trial for Leroi's murder, and not hand her over to
you and your crazy old man at all."

"You're playing with dynamite, Dannahy." I could just barely
make out a sick grin spreading across the bottom of Charlie's face as he
whispered. Abruptly, his demeanor changed, and he seemed genuinely
cheerful. "But I know you won't do that. You want that money too
badly." He slapped Dannahy on his back.

"Don't push me too far."

"Sure, sure." Charlie paused, looking around the room. His
eyes fell on me, and something occurred to him. "Besides, my good
sheriff, the person guilty of killing Leroi Cameron is lying right over
there on the floor."

Dannahy seemed fit to be tied. Then there was a deafening
banging on the doors, and he impatiently threw them open. A tall thin
youth with long red hair stammered breathlessly.

"Sh–She–Sheriff – "

"Spit it out, Davy."

"We– we–we found her, Sh–Sh–Sheriff Dannhy! She–She–
She's hold up in a ch–church d–d–down by that nigger hotel where they
were staying!"

"Well. Bring her in."

"I–I–I mean we–we couldn't get her out of there. N– Not
without p–p–permission of the head priest here in N–N–New
Orleans. The archbishop I think they c–c–call him."

"What?" Dannahy did a repeat performance of his blood-vessel
busting act.

Charlie broke in. "She's asked for sanctuary, hasn't she?"

The kid looked dumbly from Charlie to Dannahy. "Th–Th–
That's what the p–p–priest called it when we tried to get in the church."

Charlie sank down into a cross-legged position on the floor and
hid his face in his hands. Suddenly he burst out laughing.

Dannahy and the kid had no idea what was happening, much
less what Charlie found so amusing about the situation.

"What the hell? Charlie. Goddamn it, you mean to tell me –
what is this sanctuary crap anyway?"

Charlie shook his head, laughing uncontrollably.

I propped myself on my elbows, then inched my way up
against the nearest wall. "It means no civil authorities can touch her as
long as she stays inside the church."

Dannahy lunged towards me, drawing his gun barrel-first like he was going to clobber me with the butt. "You, shut up!"

Charlie waved him back. "He's right, you goddamn imbecile. I swear to Jesus, Picayune must be the only Protestant parish this close to New Orleans. You haven't ever heard of sanctuary?"

Dannahy looked back and forth between Charlie and me, not quite sure what to do.

Charlie was enjoying the whole charade. "You mean you've never read Hugo's *The Hunchback of Notre Dame*, Dannahy?"

"Note her what?"

"Never mind."

"We shall get her out of there." Everyone turned to gape at old man Damien. He'd crept up without anyone noticing him, a crafty smile on his face. "It may take a little time and a little patience, but we shall get her out of there. I guarantee it. So just relax, everyone."

After they left, locking me in that great empty vault of a room for the evening, I wracked my brain for an angle on getting out of the place and to Lucy. But there simply wasn't much I could do. My hand was so mangled, and I was so sore all over in general, it didn't seem much use in trying. I lay there for several hours, the cold floor feeling mighty good against me compared to the hot, sticky wetness of the New Orleans night. It must've been around dawn when I finally fell asleep.

I didn't get to be out for very long. They slipped in pretty soon after the sun came up, slamming the big double doors and talking in loud voices.

"There he is, ex-convict and valiant defender of the Confederacy, Santo Brady. Looking fresh and rested after a good night's sleep." It was spiteful old man Damien poised over me in a jaunty stance, a malevolent smile on his age-shrunken face. I don't know how he found out those things from my past, but I wasn't going to let him get a rise out of me.

Charlie and Dannahy showed on either side, grabbed me roughly under my arms, hoisted me in one quick motion and propped me up against the wall. I closed my eyes and almost swooned from the pain. I was seeing stars from the abrupt change of horizontal to vertical, and there was a dull throb coursing through my frame, centering itself in my left hand.

"Cat got your tongue, Mr. Brady? Not feeling quite so defiant this morning?"

Charlie laughed at his old man's jibes, then offered his own very special insight into my predicament. "I kicked all the courage out of him, and it's changed his train of thought, I can tell."

I struggled to get my eyes open and gave Charlie a poisonous look.

The old man laughed. "Mr. Brady, Doc Marleybone here –" he turned around, searching for the drunken doctor. Marleybone sheepishly skulked into the room. " – Marleybone here has impressed me greatly on your need for some kind of medication, some form of pain-deadening potion that might put you in a more receptive frame of mind towards the proposition I have to offer you."

Marleybone just stood there with a stupid, hung-over expression on his beet-red face. Old man Damien had given him his cue, and he'd flubbed it good.

"Marleybone. Wake up."

"Oh-oh, yes, Mr. Damien." He shuffled over to me, bleary-eyed, unshaven, breathing heavily. He didn't look like he was in much better shape than me. "I have some medicine for you, Brady. Guaranteed to kill the excruciating torments of a virile, manly physique that has been pushed beyond its limits. In one word: laudanum." He held up a vial and, without looking at Damien, took the water glass he offered, dumped in the contents of the vial, then stirred the contents with a grimy index finger.

"Here you are, my good fellow. Drink up. You'll be feeling as fit as a fiddle in no time at all." Something in the way Marleybone slurred his words served to produce a profound lack of confidence from me in the dope's effect. He brushed the rim of the glass against my lips. I hesitated a moment, then opened my mouth, letting him pour the whole bitter mess down my throat. Some of it ran out of my mouth and dripped off my chin.

"Good lad!" cried old man Damien, and he clapped his gnarled, arthritic hands. He made me want to puke.

As far as the laudanum went, I reckoned what the hell. I didn't give a good goddamn that they thought they could buy my cooperation with a healthy dose of narcotic. I didn't give much of a damn about anything right then. I'd had a taste of laudanum during the war when I'd been wounded and had liked how it had felt. I knew what to expect. I was looking forward to it.

"Mr. Brady, we were hoping that you might come with us and talk to Lucille, perhaps persuade her to see the error of her ways, so to speak." The old man now had a sickly affection in his voice.

The intention of his manner was calculated to convey benevolence, a sweetness borne out of the "milk of human kindness." But his phony tone, his contradictory, cruelly debased behavior towards me betrayed his calculated intentions so blatantly that, all of a sudden, I saw him for what he was. A lonely, sick old man broken by the tragedy of his life and constant heartbreak. Self-pity and decadent tastes had replaced love and understanding. He'd given up and into a terrifying emotional bankruptcy. On the outside, he'd retained a limp pretense of stalwart, uncompromising Christian morality. But inside there was nothing left… only a burnt-out, empty husk hiding from the world. And these contradictory values from his earlier life had driven him stark, raving mad.

I could see that Charlie was a lot smarter than I'd realized. He nurtured the madness in his father for his own avaricious, depraved self-interests.

The continual excruciating pain coupled with the first surge of inner narcotic warmth produced a lucidity I hadn't known since dear, sweet little Millie's death in Louisville. All of a sudden the heartbreak of Lucy's life became immeasurably clearer to me.

"Mr. Brady, will you help us talk some sense into Lucille or not?"

"What makes you think I'd even consider such a thing?"

"Because you're a selfish man, Mr. Brady. You love yourself, not my daughter. And you'd don't want to be tried for the murder of Leroi Cameron."

"Leroi Cameron was a train robber and murderer."

All of them smiled at that.

"The burden of proof is on you, Mr. Brady. In Picayune, where Mr. Cameron was released from this mortal coil, he was known as a kind, generous, upstanding citizen. Now I know you don't want to be tried and convicted of his murder, do you? You also could use a bit of money to fall back on while you recuperate from your unfortunate physical condition."

They were taking me for a real two-timing bastard. And the more I thought about it, the more I thought it would be a good idea to let them keep on heading down that primrose path. If I played my cards right, I could get in to see Lucy, and we could both start playing them off against each other.

"You don't leave me with much choice," I muttered. The opiate warmth was spreading benignly up through my stomach into my head, then down my arms and legs. Aside from a slight nausea, I was feeling wonderful.

They kept eyeing me like I was some sort of sideshow attraction… grim and anxious eyes with high expectations that I was finally breaking down, that I was going to give the word and set in motion the selling down the river of my sweetheart.

Maybe it was the drug, I don't know, but another crazy notion suddenly popped into my head. It was the kind of notion that could get me killed or engineer all their comeuppance. It occurred to me again just how much old man Damien was worth and how much Lucy and I could use that reward money. Not only could we work it so that we slipped through their greedy, grasping paws but clip them nicely for a tidy sum. Tie up the package with pretty ribbons and bows.

Barely able to focus my eyes, I smiled back at them at last.

"Hell, Mr. Damien, you've had me pegged right all along. I just don't like anybody telling me I have to do something or else. I'm a stubborn, bull-headed son-of-a-bitch that way. Now, how much cold, hard cash are we talking about?"

Before he replied, he turned to Charlie and Dannahy. "See what I told you, you two? Didn't I tell you I was a wonderful judge of human nature? And natures of some varieties of sewer rat that don't deserve the God-given privilege of being called human."

Hell, I just couldn't win. Talk about the pot calling the kettle black. He came up close to my face, close enough for me to get a whiff of his pungent, death-smelling breath. "We're speaking of five thousand dollars, Mr. Brady. I trust that will fulfill your venal needs. But fulfill them only after you have persuaded Lucille to give up this foolhardy adventure and cease her immature, adolescent behavior."

"You've got a deal, Mr. Damien."

"Fine." Then something occurred to him, and he frowned, turning to give Dannahy the evil eye. "Yes, Sheriff Dannahy, please don't say a word. I've anticipated your anxiety over the matter Mr. Brady and I have been discussing."

I glanced at Dannahy and, sure enough, the old man was right on the button. Dannahy had an unhealthy green cast to his features like maybe he was choking on something.

"I assure you, you will receive adequate remuneration for your time and Herculean efforts while in my employ." The old man, for the sake of his own health around hot-headed Dannahy, managed to keep exactly the right balance of sincerity and sarcasm.

16

By the time we arrived at St. Ambrose's Church, it was past noon. But you sure couldn't tell it from looking at the sky. Black rain clouds hung low over the entire city, blocking out the sun, creating a dreamlike atmosphere that was only intensified for me because of the laudanum.

A hulking priest with rawboned, Gallic features, ranting in a heavy Cajun patois, stood on the moss-covered stone steps. His legs were spread defiantly beneath his cassock, and he sported what resembled a heavy pirate cutlass clasped in both hands. Dannahy had gotten there ahead of the rest of us and was immersed in what I imagine he thought to be a sound, logical argument for releasing Lucy into his custody. In fact, Dannahy was so pre-occupied he didn't realize we'd arrived until our carriage pulled up right alongside him.

"Furthermore, Padre, this young woman is suspected of murder. She – "

"That'll do, my good sheriff."

Dannahy's string-bean frame jumped a yard at the sound of the old man's voice. He turned around, flushed with embarrassment at being caught in the act, pulled the hat from his head and kneaded it nervously in both hands.

"I thought that it was understood, Sheriff Dannahy, that we

were no longer employing your brand of strategy."

"I–I wanted to give it a try myself. Hell, Mr. Damien, after all we've been through, you have to admit I deserved a crack at it."

The old man glanced over at Charlie, then me, then back down to Dannahy. He leaned closer, whispering his invective to keep the priest from hearing.

"You pathetic, ignorant hillbilly. You deserved a crack at it, eh? But we've already been informed by reliable sources that the good father is a tough nut to crack. We shan't get anywhere with him, not even if we're at it for decades. We must work our persuasive wiles on Lucille, not him. And, Sheriff Dannahy, my friend, my confidant, my oh-so astute legal adviser, do you have even the foggiest notion what or who our most valuable implement of persuasion might be?"

Dannahy tore away from the old man's serpentine stare and glared at me.

"That's correct, my good sheriff, Mr. Brady is our ace in the hole." The old man swiveled his head at me and leered. "And, Mr. Brady, I pray, for your sake, that you *are* our ace. That Lucille will listen to you and your pearls of wisdom concerning her disposition."

I smiled at him. "She'll listen to me."

"Good." He turned away from me with his customarily smug, self-satisfied air and grinned at the priest who was still watching us.

I grabbed his coat-sleeve and tugged, doing my best not to lose my temper and slug him square in the face. "But before I go in, Mr. Damien, would you answer me one question?"

Suddenly nervous and no longer sure of himself, he blinked at me with trepidation. "Y-Yes?"

"Do you now or have you ever really truly loved your daughter?"

His face went purple and, all at once, I was yanked down off my seat by Charlie.

"Now, Charlie, I'd wager you're not making a very good impression on the good father here."

Charlie's eyes darted from me to the old man. Mr. Damien had already gotten his insulted pride and temper under control, so nodded his head at Charlie, motioning with one hand to ease up on the rough stuff.

I laughed at Charlie, then smiled at the priest, whose expression had changed from one of puzzlement to exasperation. Already a throng of onlookers had gathered to see what the commotion was about, what young Father "Pierre," or whatever his name was, was doing defending the church with a goddamn sword, and the wide-eyed bunch increased in number with each passing minute.

I spotted the fat Negro proprietress from the luxurious inn across the street and briefly entertained the notion of snatching Dannahy's pistol to fill her full of lead. The horse-thieving stunt I was certain she'd pulled wasn't funny to begin with, and there she was, the one who'd probably told them Lucy was in the church, snickering to herself on the sidelines.

"Father?" Old man Damien had changed his tone, speaking courteously, almost reverently.

"Yes?"

"This young gentleman," he waved his hand at me, "is an acquaintance of my daughter. Both he and I would appreciate it immensely if you could see your way clear to permit him to speak to her."

The priest shook his head with frustration. "Sir, anyone who wishes to, may enter St. Ambrose's. It is not a restricted area, nor is it a jailhouse." His French accent was doing funny things to those vowels and consonants. I knew that the old man was having to listen as carefully as me to make out what he was saying.

"Your daughter – I believe her name is Lucille? – is not a prisoner. But she has requested sanctuary in the church. And I, as a priest, must grant her that sanctuary. Anyone who wants to speak to her may speak to her, as long as it is inside the church. I'm very sorry to say this, but I know she does not want to speak to you, Mr. Damien. I know you claim to be a devout Catholic, so I am sure you are familiar with the principle of sanctuary."

It was sticking in his craw, but the old man nodded. "Father, we all only wish to alleviate the misunderstanding, the erroneous assumption that Lucille is acting under. If we can do that, if we can convince her – and I'm certain that we can – then I am confident that she will leave the protection of St. Ambrose's under her own volition and return to the bosom of her family. All of whom love her very, very much."

He'd really poured it on thick and syrupy, and I could tell that the priest was hard put knowing just what and who to believe.

"Very well, Mr. Damien." He turned his attention to me and, for the first time, spotted my banged-up condition. It was a cinch that it didn't bode well with him. He wasn't stupid and could see there was some underlying air of coercion about the whole mess. I grimaced, rolling my eyes and saw that he got the drift of what was really happening.

Nevertheless, he turned his back on them and led me up the steps into the dark, cavernous church.

17

I wasn't sure how I was going to work the money angle with them, but figured I'd lay out the whole thing for Lucy and see if she had any ideas.

The priest stalked ahead of me with long, steady strides, and I was having a hard time keeping up with him. When we came to the end of the vestibule, he opened a narrow door that creaked on century-old hinges, revealing a winding flight of crumbling stone steps.

I sagged against the wall, out of breath and near to fainting from Charlie's beating and the lack of food. He took hold of my good arm then and helped me straighten up.

"You are in worse shape than I thought."

I laughed, and it hurt to laugh.

"My name's Santo Brady, Father." I stretched out my hand. "Pleased to meet you."

He pumped it with a bear-sized paw. "I am Father Moreau. Your friends out there – they did this to you?"

"Yes."

"They aren't up to much good, are they?" His English had a naïve quality to it that made me like him.

"That is the understatement of the year."

"The old one? He is really her father?"

"I'm afraid so."

He gave me a thoughtful look, one hand stroking his broad chin.

"I don't know what kind of trouble both of you are in, but I'm afraid the extent of my help… it must be limited to the sanctuary. Outside these walls I am powerless. And if the old gentleman – "

"Mr. Damien."

"If he is as wealthy as he appears and goes to see the archbishop, I am not even certain I'll be able to help you here."

"It's like that, eh?"

He nodded grimly.

"Where is she?"

"The bell tower. Perhaps you should go first." He gracefully waved a large hand towards the stone steps, and I stumbled toward them. "Be very careful, Mr. Brady. These steps are over a hundred years old and are slick with algae from the dampness."

My head still swimming, I smiled and started the climb. There were a couple of windows in the wall looking out over the splendor of the city. I tried not to let my eyes stray because I knew the height would make me dizzy. That and the narrow, winding stair with its sharp turns were giving me butterflies in my empty stomach.

At last we reached the top. The first thing I saw when we cleared the final step was her silhouette sitting framed in an open parapet against the grey overcast sky. She didn't hear us right away, I guess because of the sound of the wind. There was an uncomfortably warm gale blowing all through the open chamber. She was staring out over the blocks of buildings behind the church, so I knew she was probably unaware of the whole scene that had been played when we'd pulled up.

"Lucy."

She spun around like someone had shot her, then was on her feet running to me. She fell into my arms, clasping me snug around my shoulders and pressing her soft, fragrant lips into mine.

"Santo! How did you ever find me?"

I glanced at Moreau, and he fidgeted away, caught somewhere between pity and embarrassment. "I'll take leave of you."

I called after him as he reached the stairwell. "Father, I hope you won't think me too rude, but do you have any food? Anything at all? I'm ready to drop."

"I can bring you a loaf of bread, perhaps a bit of cheese, a little wine…"

"Fine. Anything is fine."

He nodded and headed back down the steps.

Again I looked into Lucy's eyes. They were searching mine. She was trying to understand where she stood.

"How did I find you? Your father and brother told me. They led me right to the very doorstep of this church."

She was shocked.

"Didn't Father Moreau tell you that Dannahy's men had been here?"

She gasped. "No."

"He's a nice fellow. I guess he didn't want to alarm you."

She kept her arms around me, clinging even tighter. Standing on her tiptoes to look over my shoulder, she kept watch on the door that led downstairs.

"I can't understand why he didn't tell me they were here. He won't turn me in, will he?" It was more a statement of fact than a question but, even still, I could tell she was terribly frightened, or she wouldn't've mentioned it.

"No. You're under the protection of the Church by right of sanctuary."

She nodded, her expression blank.

"Well, I don't know how they did it, but they found you. It may've been that fat bitch from our flophouse accommodations across the street. They got to me on the riverboat. Your brother, Charlie, had on a deputy sheriff's badge, so he didn't have any trouble convincing the other upstanding citizens he was within his rights when he dragged me off."

She slowly sank to her knees, her face a frozen, ashen mask, every ounce of emotion erased by shock and exhaustion. I kneeled down beside her.

"Honey." I shook her, and she looked dully up at me. "We've got to figure out what we're going to do quick. Your father sent me up here to bring you down – " I laughed, " – talk some 'sense' into your head and persuade you to go home with them."

"What?"

"I lied to him. He's willing to pay me off big to sweet-talk you out of here. He knows he can't touch you. At least not right away."

Suddenly she realized how badly I was beaten up.

"Santo, what've they done to you?" She held one of her hands against my throbbing head while stretching the other to delicately touch my bandaged, mangled hand.

"Our good pal, Charlie, really worked me over. Unfortunately I had to just lie there and take it."

She pulled me over to the parapet, and we sat down. I accidentally caught a glimpse of the vast height, the buildings below us seeming so small they might as well have been doll houses, and I started to black out. She yanked me to her as I wavered, jolting me back to consciousness with surprising strength.

"How much money did he say he'd give you?"

"Five thousand. But he's not going to cough it up until he's got his hands on you."

"You mean his shackles." She thought for a minute, her face knotted with lines of concentration. When it came to her, her face suddenly relaxed, and she laughed. "You do exactly what I say. We'll wrangle the money from the old goat and get the hell out of here at the same time." She pulled me closer and whispered her plan in my ear.

18

Father Moreau came back with a stale loaf of dark rye, no cheese and a bitter tasting red wine. I thanked him and immediately devoured the meager supper. I then explained our plan, that it was somewhat duplicitous but wouldn't require him to do anything illegal. That is if he decided to cooperate. He gave it careful thought, then proceeded to detail the shortcomings of Lucy's proposed escape route. His description of the cellars and catacombs beneath the church was harrowing. But he wasn't overly pessimistic and allowed that we might perhaps succeed if our timing was right and he was a good enough actor to cover our tracks.

The bread and wine revived me a bit and, once Father Moreau had reluctantly promised his help, I descended the precarious stairs to confront the old man.

Charlie and Dannahy were both leaning against separate wheels of the carriage when I came out of the church. Both had their arms folded and ludicrously sullen expressions of pent-up frustration on their faces. The old man was napping on the crushed velvet seat. He was snoring loudly, his head thrown gracelessly back over a brocaded, cushioned headrest.

I tapped him on the knee, and he started.

"Well?" He barked impatiently, flushed and sweaty from sleep.

"She wouldn't come."

"You weren't convincing enough. She saw right through you."

"No, the story I gave her was convincing enough. I told her you only wanted to see her in the flesh, talk to her yourself. And if you couldn't convince her to come home with you, you would let her go and never bother her again."

"Yes?" He was perched on the edge of his seat, hanging on my every word.

"She wanted to think it over. She doesn't trust you at all."

I guess Charlie wasn't as frustrated as I'd thought because he chuckled from where he'd planted himself beside me. The old man didn't find any humor in the situation and glared at him.

"You'd better hope for your sake, Mr. Brady, that she decides to believe the both of us."

I shrugged. His implied threats were getting tiresome.

Charlie put in his two cents. "I think she'll come around."

Then something happened that I knew could either insure our plan's success or throw a herd of horseflies in the buttermilk.

Somehow a Federal Marshal had come on the scene.

Somebody, probably some busybody derelict from the crowd, had filled him in, and now he was determined to get to the bottom of the whole sordid affair.

Duded up in a grey tweed suit and red satin vest, he cut a striking figure, and the gold badge he wore was so polished it was blinding people. He didn't have a gun hanging on his hip, but I could tell from the bulge under his coat that he was definitely armed.

"Hello, gentlemen, I'm Marshal Amos Jennings. What seems to be the trouble here?"

An obnoxiously phony smile contorted the old man's face, and he stretched out his hand.

"No trouble at all, Marshal. My name's Edward Damien. I'm from St. Louis, and I'm trying desperately to contact my daughter who has run away from home. She's sought refuge in the church here."

"Is that right?" The Marshal matched him in the phony smile department, if that was possible. His mustachioed, line-creased face studied each of us – Dannahy, Charlie, me, the scum that made up Dannahy's posse and the son-of-a-bitch old man. He took off his flat, wide brim preacher's hat and scratched the wild, unmanageable bush of red hair that covered his huge head. He towered over all of us except Charlie, who was actually able to look him in the eye.

Charlie made a split-second judgment on his formidable adversary and decided to mimic his father. "I'm Charlie Damien. I'm very pleased to make your acquaintance, Marshal Jennings. We've been searching high and low for my sister for the last couple of years. And I'm happy to say we've finally found her."

"You don't say."

I could see he was inspecting their badges – Charlie's, then Dannahy's and then the rest of the sorry, misbegotten crew.

"Uh, hunh, I see. Who's in charge here?"

Dannahy was only too glad to acknowledge some kind of responsibility and get his sticky fingers back in the pie. "I am, Marshal." He stretched out his hand. "Sheriff Ross Dannahy from Picayune, Mississippi."

Jennings didn't take his hand. "A little outside your jurisdiction, aren't you, Sheriff?"

Dannahy looked like a balloon that somebody'd let the air out of – deflated and shrunken. His hand fell to his side like a rock. He hemmed and hawed.

"Well, uh, I , er… I've been retained by, uh – "

Charlie butted in, "Sheriff Dannahy has been of invaluable assistance to us. He's investigating a murder that occurred in Picayune and has reason to believe that my sister, Lucille, was the only witness."

I couldn't believe my ears. Going out of his way to save Dannahy's ass was not in Charlie's character. I tried not to laugh as I saw the smug expression of self-interest spread across his face. Old man Damien had on the same look – two peas in a pod.

"Do you have extradition papers, Sheriff?"

All of them fell silent. Once he saw they had no intention of answering his perfectly reasonable questions, Jennings finally noticed me.

"Who are you?"

"Santo Brady." I smiled up at the old man and added, "A friend of Miss Damien."

Jennings could tell right away that I was on Lucy's side and not trying to put on some kind of show to impress him.

"Tell me, Mr. Brady, how old is this Miss Damien?"

"21 years old."

He turned to the old man. "Sounds as if she's of age, sir. Old enough to make up her own mind without undue coercion."

"I assure you, Marshal, no force nor coercion has entered into the picture."

"That's good, Mr. Damien. I'm glad to hear it. Especially since the young lady in question found it necessary to seek sanctuary in St. Ambrose's." He turned to me again. "Mr. Brady, would you be good enough to accompany me inside? I should like to meet Miss Damien."

19

When we got inside the church, I gave the Marshal the entire story, from how Lucy and I'd met, her leaving the convent, from crazy, murdering Charlie to Leroi's train robbery, from Lucy killing him to the whole bunch coming after us. Lucy killing Leroi didn't bother him in the least. He knew who Leroi was, knew he'd had a good price on his head. He thought Lucy had done humanity a great service and wondered why the hell we hadn't collected the reward. Of course. what he really wanted to know was why they were all after us. He understood that with the old man, it wanting his daughter back. But he knew there had to be some other reason for the rest of them to be so goddamn interested. I told him that Dannahy and probably Charlie thought we had the train money and were determined to wrest it from us. When I lied for the first time and told him we'd never had the money and didn't have the faintest idea what had become of it… well, for the first time he looked at me funny. I knew he'd believed everything else up to that point. That last little bit he wasn't sure about.

"Maybe you've better let me talk to Miss Damien."

We climbed the steep narrow steps to the belfry and found Father Moreau hearing Lucy's confession. I'd heard of that strange Catholic rite before but nevertheless was shocked to see Lucy kneeling in her torn red dress, eyes closed and hands folded, whispering prayers while Father Moreau sat there making odd gestures with his hands.

The Marshal held back, polite and courteous, and took off his hat.

When they finished, they both stood up and approached us.

"Lucy, Father Moreau, this is Marshal Jennings. He's trying to straighten things out."

Without tipping our hand, Lucy gave me a curious look.

"Hello, Father, pleased to meet you." He shook Moreau's hand, then turned to Lucy. "Miss Damien?"

"Yes, sir." She smiled demurely and curtsied. Even though her hair was tangled and her clothes caked with dirt, I'd never seen her more charming, more hypnotically attractive.

I saw that the Marshal was blushing. "Ma'am, pleased to meet you, I'm sure. Mr. Brady here has filled me in on the details of this thing. I take it you've requested sanctuary her at St. Ambrose's because of your father and the men with him?"

She shyly nodded.

"I see. Well, the one thing I need to be absolutely sure of if I'm to intercede in this matter – I mean, you're perfectly secure in St. Ambrose's as long as you stay inside – but I could possibly offer you safe conduct from the city if you answer me one question, and I am satisfied with the answer."

"Yes?"

"Mr. Brady has mentioned to me this whole business about Leroi Cameron and the train robbery. I understand you had to dispatch Mr. Cameron – in self-defense, of course. But what I don't know, beyond Mr. Brady's assurances, is what became of the monies taken in that robbery."

She glanced at me, trying to figure just what it was she was supposed to say.

"Is this some kind of trick question, Marshal?"

"No, Ma'am, not at all. I would just appreciate hearing the truth from you. And if it matches up with what Mr. Brady has told me, then I think I might be of service to you."

"Marshal, Mr. Brady and I never ever laid eyes on that money. If any of my Father's associates outside are under the impression that we have that money with us, they are gravely mistaken."

She was convincing as hell, and I could tell that the Marshal believed her.

"That's all I wanted to know."

He stepped to one of the open spaces in the wall and stared down at the small crowd outside the church. He was a big fellow with a self-confident demeanor and cocky swagger that was infectious. But I knew from the way he was working his hat, turning it over and over in his hands, that he was nervous. He was uneasy about Damien and the ragamuffin posse below.

"Something wrong, Marshal?"

Not looking at me, he answered with a sigh. "I don't know why it is, but I've got a bad feeling about this. It seems like it should be a pretty simple situation to handle… but… I don't know." He shook his head.

It was getting dark. Smoke rose from the street below, and I joined him to study the neighborhood, careful to not get too close to the edge because of my vertigo. The smoke was from torches. Fifteen or twenty men had gathered around the old man's carriage. I could make out both Charlie and Dannahy circulating amongst them, stirring up a commotion. A short fat man appeared out of an alley with a pack of dogs.

"The old bastard. He's really overdoing things."

"It looks like he's going to give me trouble, doesn't it?"

I stared him in the eye and nodded grimly. "He's hiring himself some more guns right now."

He turned to Moreau. "Father, could I speak to you for a moment?"

Moreau seemed a little startled that he was actually being consulted about something. He followed Jennings out and down the steps.

Lucy timidly came up behind me, peeking over my shoulder to survey the scene below. She was being careful, making sure no one could spot her. There were several men, Marleybone amongst them, taking time out from passing a jug around to point up at us.

Suddenly, with a deafening pulse in my head, my bad hand convulsed like it was exploding. For a split second, I thought maybe someone from down there had shot me. Everything went black, and Lucy had to grab me with both hands, spinning me towards her to keep me from plummeting to my death. We both toppled backwards, and I came down heavily on top of her. She crawled out from underneath me and held my head in her lap.

"Santo, Santo!"

I tried to speak but nothing would come. I pointed to my bandaged hand, and she gently picked it up. Even her tender, delicate touch stabbed through me, and I cried out. She slowly unraveled the yellowed, evil-smelling strips of cloth. The last strands stuck to my palm, and Lucy's eyes went wide. She averted them, turning her head and clapping one hand over her mouth to keep from being sick. I realized then that Marleybone had been telling me the truth about the hand.

"It's going to have to come off, isn't it?"

She didn't want to look me in the eye because she knew that she couldn't lie about something like that. She was smart enough to know that if my hand didn't come off, pretty soon the localized virulence would be coursing through every inch of me.

"Oh sweet Jesus, Santo." She gently lay my hand on the floor then ran over to a bundle she had stashed in the corner. I could see her getting out a bottle of whiskey.

"Have you still got that Peacemaker in there?"

"Yes?"

"Bring it, too."

She leapt the distance between us then was crouching by my side again. I tried to see her through the haze that was suddenly clouding up my vision. I wasn't sure because my eyelids were squeezed nearly shut from the pain, but it looked like there were tears running all down her cheeks. She pulled the cork on the bottle and slopped about a fifth of it onto the swollen, yellow-purple pulp of my hand. I was so far gone I couldn't even feel it. No burning, no stabbing, no blast furnace going off inside my head. Just a slight stinging, then a dead, numb nothingness that scared the hell out of me.

She pressed the bottle to my lips, and I sucked it up like a baby at its mother's breast. The liquor ran through me like fire, and suddenly, miraculously my head cleared. All at once I could hear Lucy, what she was saying, and realized she wasn't talking to me at all. She was praying.

She tore several strips of cloth and wound them around my hand.

The whiskey did another jig inside my head, and I pushed my way up to a sitting position, grabbing at her, kissing her all over her tear-stained face and telling her in hoarse, hurting whispers how much I loved her. Her mouth was hot and wet against mine as she kissed me back. Then she pulled away, brushing her lips against my cheeks and forehead, and finally my burning eyes, lingering on them with a feverish reverie.

I don't know where I found the strength – I reckon it must've been from her – but I stood up as straight and steady as I could and drew her up with me.

Then somebody tapped me on the shoulder, and I whirled around with Lucy's Peacemaker and her still in my arms, ready to kill.

It was the Marshal with Father Moreau standing beside him.

"We've got a pretty severe mob scene on our hands, you two. Father Moreau told me about your plan of getting out through the catacombs beneath the church. I think it is a good idea."

Three shadows stirred behind them, and I heard the hammer of a pistol being cocked. Then there they were – Dannahy, Charlie and the old man. All three of them were grinning like they'd just won some great big poker game in the sky.

"Lucille, my dear – " The old man actually sounded like he was getting sentimental.

"Hello, sister." Charlie said it liltingly, chock full of sarcasm and swagger.

"You're going to regret this." Marshall Jennings sobered them up with his steady, icy voice. The rest of us didn't say anything. Lucy sighed and buried her face in my chest so she didn't have to look at them.

Dannahy was the one who had his gun drawn, a polished Colt .45 with engraved ivory handles. A little rich for a farmer-turned-bounty hunter's blood. But bounty hunter was the key word.

The three of them smiled again, the same reptilian smile like they were each part of the same scaly monster.

Charlie brought something up from his side and, once it came more into the fading twilight, I recognized the gargantuan bullwhip that Lucy had described.

The old man stepped forward and lay a palsied hand on Father Moreau's shoulder. "I do regret this, Father Moreau, for your sake. I know you feel you've been trying to do your duty. But I'm afraid my daughter is in need of discipline – on a physical as well as spiritual plane."

Lucy exploded with fury. "Goddman you, Papa! How dare you judge me. You'd better look in the mirror first, then pray to Jesus for forgiveness. Hope and pray He'll show you some kind of mercy to wash away all the blood on your hands."

The old man was a little taken aback in spite of himself.

"I've missed you profoundly, Lucille." He'd changed his tone even more, and, for the first time – at least in my memory – his voice cracked with honest emotion. "Your place is at home in St. Louis – back with us and back with the Ursulines."

Her mouth was agape in shock. I knew she was struggling against the tiny spark of natural feeling she still held for her father. But too much of that love and affection had been doused then buried beneath the dirt of his hypocrisy, his self-deluding pride and maniacal self-righteousness.

"I'm never ever going back. You'll have to kill me first."

"Move aside, Marshal." Dannahy nudged him with his gun barrel. With his free hand, he reached beneath the Marshal's suitcoat and plucked the revolver from his shoulder holster. He pointed with his gun at a lantern hanging on the wall beside one of the open spaces. It was getting a little too dark. "Light it, Marshal. And don't try anything funny, or I'll splatter your puny set of brains all over our captive audience below."

The old man didn't like that kind of talk, especially in the church, and reprimanded him. "I don't have any use for your chest-pounding or less-than-eloquent braggadocio, my good Sheriff. So you will kindly cease and desist with your proclamations."

I could see that Dannahy wasn't getting any happier about taking guff off the old man. Not in the least. He was rapidly reaching the end of his long and frayed rope. But he knew the right moment hadn't arrived yet. He still had to toe the line. And like it.

The old man did an about face with his demeanor, smiling up at the stocky bulwark of Father Moreau. "Father, please sit down here. You don't appear very comfortable." The old man nodded to Charlie. Charlie steered Moreau into a seat against the wall then turned back to the Marshal.

"You, too, Marshal. Except I'm afraid you'll have to stand. It seems we've run out of chairs." A nasty smile spread across his face as Marshal Jennings grudgingly took his place beside Moreau.

With more light in the chamber, Dannahy noticed the gun in my hand.

"Hand it over, Brady."

Lucy took it from me, then holding it in both hands and aiming it at Dannahy, she teasingly cocked the hammer.

Dannahy went white as Lucy spoke. "I swear to God if you don't, all of you, get the hell out of here, I'm going to blow your heads off."

Dannahy gave a nervous laugh, not sure what to do. Charlie and the old man looked scared of her.

"Put down that gun, my child. You are courting disaster."

"Stay out of this, Father Moreau." She gave him a quick sidelong glance that chilled my blood, then once again concentrated on Dannahy.

Marshal Jennings, fidgeting in place and unable to bear the tension any longer, stepped forward. "I'm telling you both for the last time – put down your weapons."

While the Marshal briefly had her attention, Charlie lashed out with his whip, and it snaked around her arms. He heaved backwards, she went spinning, and as the gun flew from her grasp, it went off, drilling Marshal Jennings squarely through the heart. With an incredulous look on his face, Jennings collapsed and sprawled out dead on the stone floor.

I dove for Lucy's gun as it fell and was covering Dannahy before anyone could say a word.

Lucy picked herself up, muttering curses at Charlie. "You filthy son-of-a-bitch. You no-good bastard."

Charlie stared at her blankly. He wasn't stupid. He knew killing a U.S. Marshal was a federal crime, and he stood there pre-occupied with the enormity of his mistake. The wheels were going around inside his head, undoubtedly trying to piece together how he could shove off the blame onto somebody else – probably me. He knew that his old man would never let either him or Lucy assume the guilt. Unfortunately there was another witness besides me and Lucy – the priest.

Moreau stooped down to Jennings' corpse, and Dannahy grabbed the opportunity he'd been waiting for, cocking his pistol.

I fired twice, catching him once in the stomach, once in the throat. He wavered in place for a few seconds, not quite comprehending what had happened to him. He tried to aim his gun as he coughed up a handful of blood. But his hand was shaking badly, and the weapon was caked with the red stuff.

"Y-Y-You – bas-bastard." His words were a strangled whisper, barely recognizable as a human voice. With one final effort, he squeezed the trigger. The gun exploded from the sticky mess that covered it, and the impact blew off his fingers. His whole body jerked backwards, and he plummeted out of the open space down to the church steps. It was a good drop. Immediately there was a bloodcurdling uproar from the crowd.

Charlie cracked his whip again, this time at me, but missed my gun by inches. I let him have it in the hand, and he yelped, grabbing his palm and dropping the whip like it was a hot andiron.

"I'll kill you for that!" His face was disfigured with rage.

"Not today." I smiled, covering him and the old man while Lucy got her bundle of stuff and Jennings' gun that still lay on the floor.

The old man looked grim but didn't say anything, just stared out into the smoky night.

"You're forgetting something aren't you, Mr. Damien?"

He turned to face me, but his eyes remained blank.

I walked over to him, reached under his coat to its inside pockets. The one on the right turned up nothing but a folded sheaf of documents. But from the left one I pulled out his wallet. I pried it open and found a folded pack of twenty fifties.

"This isn't quite what we agreed on." I tucked it in my pants pocket and threw the empty wallet in his face. "But it'll do."

Moreau stood up, shaking his head sadly.

"C'mon, Father."

He gave me a questioning look, then realized what I was talking about.

"Yes, you two don't have very long before they're all up here. Follow me."

He quickly walked out and down, and we backed after him, still keeping a bead on Charlie and the old man. Once we were on the steps, Lucy banged the heavy door shut then bolted it.

I could hear the crowd striking at the church gates and realized that they must've thought they were locked.

Moreau stopped on one of the slightly wider steps before we reached bottom and pushed open a narrow strip of a door that I hadn't spotted.

"You're on your own now." Disgusted at the bloodshed, he petulantly slammed the door behind us and locked it, throwing us into complete darkness.

20

The passage was very narrow and, since I was still woozy, I let Lucy take the lead. An aroma of dankness and decay, of slimy wet stone that had never seen the light of day, overpowered us.

Lucy gave out a wheezing rasp. "I can barely breathe."

"Keep moving, honey. And if you're going to talk at all, whisper."

We had to walk sideways because of the closed-in space, and the slime came off on our clothes.

"Hell, Santo, we should've brought a lantern."

I tried to make a joke out of it. "When I'm rushed, I forget things." I stumbled clumsily against an uneven stone. "We've got to really watch our step – it could drop off any place along here."

Abruptly we came to a corner and collided into each other. She reached down somewhere, then I heard her rustling in the bundle.

"I think I've got some matches in here." A few more seconds ticked by, and she struck one. A ribbon of corridor about thirty feet long came into view.

Already there was an awful racket starting behind us, and I imagined that the crowd had probably already made it up the steps to the bell tower. In a matter of moments, Charlie and the old man would figure out where we'd gone. Then we'd really have something to worry about.

Suddenly the match went out, and a rambunctious squawking welled up around us.

"Santo, there're rats in here!"

"Keep your voice down. There's nothing we can do about the rats. Keep moving."

I could tell she was having difficulty navigating in the darkness, especially with the rats starting to swarm around our feet. To make things worse, the vaulted space, the uneven floor, had made our footsteps into deafening blasts and had somehow picked up the echo of the bloodthirsty bunch upstairs.

Lucy lit another match, and the rats scattered. I could see a sharp decline ahead, then the floor disappearing after a short stretch in stagnant water. Beyond that the corridor seemed to widen quite a bit. The match lasted till the edge of the water, and we both paused again.

We were both getting pretty frantic because we weren't making much headway. And now Lucy was hesitating because of the water. The rats came back as soon as the light was gone, and I knew all of it was starting to pile up on her. Pile up on me, too, for that matter. It was giving me the willies. I goosed her, and she gave out with a nervous laugh.

"We can't stop, honey. I don't think they've made it into the passage yet. But once they do, you can bet they'll have torches and maybe dogs, and it'll only take a matter of minutes for them to catch up to us."

I kissed her in the dark, and she nodded against my cheek.

She moved away from me, splashing across the cold, evil-smelling stuff, and I followed. From there on we ran blindly ahead for another ten or twenty yards.

We were getting to the point where we were memorizing the lighted stretch in front of us every time she lit a match, and it was helping us to move faster.

She took a half-step as she lit another one and tripped forward. I grabbed out for her, catching her around the waist. The match fell from her hand, disappearing into a chasm about three feet across and God knows how many feet deep. We inched slowly backwards.

"We're going to have to jump it."

She was trembling against me. I knew she didn't think much of the idea, but she said, "Okay."

I felt a big rat brush against my ankle, and it gave me an idea. I kicked out at it hoping I could knock it into the hole. The kick connected, the thing squealed, and for a couple of seconds I wasn't sure if it had landed in the hole or not. Then there was a splash – the time between my kick and the sound of the water told me the hole was deep. Deep enough so that if either of us fell into it, we'd need some help getting out. If we were still alive to get out.

I edged us both back about six feet or so.

"Light another match so I can see where we are."

She lit one.

"Here, give it to me."

She handed it over, and I held it up high.

"Now, get your running start and jump."

She gave me an uncertain look, shrugged, then bolted away from me and over the hole. She slipped on the slimy floor as she came down on the other side and scraped her hands against the slick green wall to keep her balance.

My match went out. She lit another immediately, and I ran and leapt without hesitation. I bumped into her, and the light went out.

"I've only got one more left."

"Save it then, till we really need it. I think I can remember how it looked for twenty feet or so. But take it easy – no telling if there's more holes along here like that one."

We continued, me in the lead taking short, quick steps, feeling along the wall with my good hand. My shakiness hadn't gone away – the punishment I'd been through, the lack of food and sleep, the pulsing infection that was my hand, all of it was dragging me down. At least the dizziness hadn't gotten any worse. I kept plodding on, trying not to think any further than the next step. I suppose it was knowing that there wasn't one single alternative for her or me but to keep going. Or else just lie down and die. It was getting to the point where we were each holding the other one up. If either she or I had been alone, we wouldn't've stood half a chance. And we wouldn't've had the stamina, the endurance to make the never-ending haul to freedom. It was a long way. In both a real and figurative sense, we still couldn't make out any light at the end of the tunnel.

I came to a sharp corner and stopped. She clutched at me, letting out a deep sigh.

I put my arm around her. "Getting tired?"

"No, I'm all right."

We rounded the bend together, and for the first time down there, I felt a cool breeze fan my perspiring face.

"We must be close."

All of a sudden we were able to pick up speed. It wasn't utter blackness anymore – there was a faint glow up ahead, and the darkness was giving way to grey light.

I turned to Lucy and was surprised to see the silhouette of her profile.

"What do we do when we get to the cemetery?" I knew she'd detailed things to Moreau, but I didn't think he'd had time to do anything about it.

"I don't know. Father Moreau was supposed to have horses waiting at a spot near where the tunnel spills into the graveyard. But then those sons-of-bitches surprised us, and he didn't have time. I hope the mob isn't one step ahead of us and waiting there."

"They couldn't be." I tried to reassure her, but my tone of voice gave me away – it quivered, a whisper barely coming at all. "We're close enough. Let's light that last match."

She did as I told her, and the tunnel flared into a garish orange light. She gasped. Right before our eyes was gruesome proof why the tunnel was called a catacomb. For maybe ten yards on either side of us there were recesses in the wall. Open, unsealed oblong spaces, six or seven at a time stacked atop one another. Rotting and exposed cadavers lay unprotected in the rock crannies, their burial shrouds having long ago decayed and crumbled into dust. They were skeletons for the most part, with only one or two sporting a scaly parchment of dry, dead flesh.

I recognized the musty smell then and knew if for what it was – Death.

21

When we at last reached the end of the passage, I was surprised at how little light there was. Then I saw the partition covering the entrance from outside. Lucy pushed against it, and it broke apart at the touch. The door collapsed into several uneven pieces of rotting timber. The opening of the crypt or tomb or whatever the hell it was we were inside of had been recessed into the wall, leaving a long forgotten alcove. A curtain of ivy and Spanish moss proved an almost impenetrable tangle between the alcove and the outside world.

Lucy threw up her hands.

I didn't know what to say. I was trying to think what would be our best course of action when an idea occurred to me on how I could maybe slow down the posse. I gave Lucy my gun and picked up several sections of the splintered, worm-eaten door with my good hand.

"Stay here and don't make a sound, honey. If I'm not back in five minutes, get the hell out of here."

I started back down the tunnel at a fast clip, estimating the distance we'd come from that abyss in the floor. After I turned the first corner, I slowed. Ahead of me, I could hear the sound of them trampling closer. They were going all out hell-for-leather at breakneck pace. Their angry, drunken voices and the baying of hounds echoed eerily through the stone labyrinth and made the hair stand up on the back of my neck. I had to act fast.

I didn't have any more matches, so I used the boards as feelers out in front of me, tapping the slippery rock like a blind man would use his cane. Suddenly the boards lurched forward into open space, and I almost dropped them into the chasm. I quickly knelt and placed the flimsy planks lengthwise as best I could over the opening. Torches or not, if they came barreling down the tunnel fast enough, I knew that two or three of them in the lead would smash through the boards and fall into my trap. I figured it'd slow them down at least a good ten minutes – probably more if the hole was as deep as I thought.

I turned and raced back as fast as I could.

When I got to the spot where I'd left Lucy, I thought at first she hadn't done what I'd told her. I stealthily moved to the edge of the hanging vines, then froze. Whispering voices were coming from the other side. One of the voices was hers, the other I wasn't sure of, but it had the tonal quality of an elderly man. I peeked through, parting the damp, clinging strands to get a better look.

"Sho' 'nough, Missy… Fatha' Moreau send me." It was an old, white-bearded Negro clad in tattered clothes. He sat atop a crude wagon pulled by a broken down, flea-bitten pair of mules.

"He didn't tell me anything about you."

"Josephus, missy. I'm the custodian of Saint Ambrose. Fatha' Morea sho' 'nough send me jes the same. You bes' be quick if'n you want t'get out of town 'head dat mob."

Lucy had him covered with her pistol, and he seemed pretty comfortable about it, all things considered. Which could stand us in good stead if we got stopped along the way. I came through into the grey light of the newly risen moon, and he didn't flinch one bit. In fact, he acted like he'd expected me.

"Here yo' fren', Missy. Come 'long now, else you sho' gone be sorry." He twisted, leaning over backwards to pull away the tarpaulin that lay bunched on the wagon bed.

Lucy looked at me, and I nodded.

"What've we got to lose?"

She smiled as she climbed into the wagon. I swung up beside her and helped the old man pull the tarpaulin over us. It was a foul-smelling piece of canvas, probably from some slaughterhouse, stiff with dried grease and blood. The stench and the closeness of it made me retch, and I propped myself to lean over the side so I wouldn't be sick on the both of us. I'd backslid again from resolute strength to dizzying sickness.

Lucy steadied one hand against my spine. The warmth of her palm through my torn shirt helped bring me back from the brink of unconsciousness. She and Josephus covered us, and we were off.

The mules' lackadaisical pace made a gentle clip-clopping on the stone lane and the rickety wagon wheels clattered in time to it.

I turned away from Lucy onto my right side so as not to put any pressure on my left arm. She snaked her arms around my chest, holding me snug. She held her face close to the back of my head, and I could feel her hot breath coming in short gasps against my neck.

"I love you, Santo."

I closed my eyes. I felt like crying. I fought the tears, but a couple rolled down my flushed, feverish cheeks. That's when I started thinking again. And the thinking left the door wide open for fear to come creeping up on me, ganging up with the burning yellow sickness in my hand to choke me, to throttle the very life right out of me. I trembled uncontrollably, and no matter how tightly Lucy held me to her, the tremors would not go away.

"Santo, darling, I'm here. I'm going to take care of you. We'll get out of this, I know it."

I couldn't speak. I couldn't even nod my head. I was paralyzed with a fright I'd never known before. I had to somehow steer my mind off its one-track bent. I started looking for something, anything to divert my attention – a trick that I could play on my mind to send the pendulum of dread swinging back the other way.

Peering between the slats on my side of the wagon bed, I could make out the tombs and crypts that scurried by us. They were above ground for the most part and, as anyone who's been to New Orleans knows, fashioned after houses. But these squat, narrow houses with their baroque and classical designs were so tiny, so close that even a child could see that they weren't houses at all. At least not for the living. They were houses of the dead – some built cozy and snug enough for just one poor soul, and some engineered with a spectacular flourish to accommodate a whole family of cadavers.

There was one in particular with marble walls and pillars, stained glass windows and a roof covered with a moss nearly obscured by drooping cypress branches. It stuck in my mind long after we'd passed it, and I imagined it blown up a hundred times its true size. I saw it perched on a forgotten island deep in the most treacherous swamp. I saw Lucy living with me in it – far removed from the threat of war or strangling family ties.

With my eyes closed, Lucy's hot, quick breath against my neck painted a picture of us in bed together in a vaulted, high-ceilinged bedroom.

"You there, old man! Stop the wagon!"

The gruff, blustery voice had come out of nowhere from up ahead of us.

"Why, it's old Josephus from St. Ambrose." Yet another voice – higher-pitched and more nasal than the first.

Remaining hidden, Lucy raised herself a few inches, peeked under Josephus' seat, then cuddled back up to me.

"There's just two of them."

"What you doin' out here in the graveyard, old man?" It was a deep-voiced fellow, and his manner was more threatening than the other one.

"I ain't but comin' on home from puttin' flowehs on Monsignor Ch-Chardin's tomb." He stammered, pronouncing the CH harsh and without the French accent, and it made the nasally-sounding man laugh. However, his friend meant business and went on interrogating Josephus with a nasty, self-important tone.

"You used t'work out at Duvall's place a few years back."

"Dat was befo' de war, suh. Befo' I 'came a freed man."

"Yessirree! I 'member you. Always getting' inna mischief with the ladies – "

Josephus laughed nervously. "I can't say I recall anyt'ing in particular, Cap'n, but – "

"All right, boy. Cut the bullshit. We lookin' fo' an 'scaped murderer. Crazy fella who kit-napped a woman an' kilt Father Moreau, Marshall Jennings and a sheriff from Mississippi. Kilt 'em in col' blood. Shot 'em down like'n they's dogs."

Lucy clutched at me when he said Moreau's name. I was pretty shocked that they'd killed him. It seemed like her father would've drawn the line at killing a priest. Then again, Charlie didn't have any such qualms. With Dannahy dead, all the arrows certainly pointed to him.

"'Taint seen hide no' hair a no mur'drers, Cap'n."

"We came 'round this way to the cemetery to head 'em off. They had to've gotten out the church through the cat'combs. And the cat'combs lead to only one place. Right here."

"Cat-what?"

"Harry, you wastin' yo' time. This ig'nant nigger don' know a blasted thing."

Lucy squeezed me tighter as the man called Harry started to circle the wagon.

"Then why he comin' from the cemetery, him bein' from St. Ambrose an' all?"

"You gotta point, Harry."

"What you carryin', Uncle?"

"Not a blessed thing, Cap'n." Josephus was getting nervous, I could tell from his voice. And if I could tell, I knew those two nosy sons-of-bitches –

"It look like you got somethin' under the tarp here, Uncle."

"Not nothin' under that tarp."

The nasally one's footsteps came around and joined Harry. They both stopped at the rear of the wagon. Lucy let go of me, aiming the gun as one of them lifted the tarp. Before they could even make eye-contact with us, she pulled the trigger twice. Harry went down with a bullet in the middle of his bewhiskered face. The nasally one yelled, fell backwards clutching his gun arm, but stayed on his feet. Josephus reined in on his startled mules to stop the wagon from jerking back and forth.

"You! Why'd you shoot us, girl? We tryin' to do nothin' but rescue you!" He was crying with a high-pitched whine tears streaming down his face.

"I don't need rescuing. I'm trying to get away from those men. I'm trying to get away from that rich old bastard who's paying your wages."

"Harry an' me ain't been paid a red cent. We only wanted to see justice done again' a col'-blooded killer."

"This fella here hasn't killed anyone. My brother Charlie killed all three of those men. Remember that when you see them again."

"Missy, you gone leave him 'live an' kickin'?" Josephus didn't like the idea, and I was inclined to agree with him.

She nodded, staring coldly at the whimpering, wounded man. "Get going, Josephus."

"If'n you say so, Missy." He yanked at the reins, then lashed out at the confused mules with his whip. The wagon jolted forwards.

The man slowly dropped to his knees beside his partner, staring after us with his eyes full of hate. "Damn you to hell, girl!"

I sank back onto the rollicking wagon bed. The tensions in Lucy's frail body seeped away. She gradually held herself less rigid. And, as the wagon bucked with each crack in the cobblestone pavement, her frame became like a limp rag doll. Finally she stopped gazing behind us and lay down beside me. She pulled the tarpaulin cover back up over us just as lightning burnt through the sky and rain started to fall.

"Ain't gonna be long, you two, an' we be headed out dis boneyard. Dis place got a curse on itself, sho' 'nough."

The rain pelted through the covering, liquefying the rancid grease and cow's blood until we were soaked with it. Lucy nestled against my cheek, holding my face against hers with one hand until the smell of blood and grease was banished by the perfume of her sweating skin. I fell asleep while I was kissing her. The next thing I knew, we were deep in the country on the outskirts of New Orleans.

22

The road out of that hell was a big blur to me. I guess I must've been delirious, because I don't recall too much of it. I know we stopped in Baton Rouge to change the mules to a couple of horses. Lucy paid for them. I'll never know how we made it that far out of New Orleans at such a snail's pace without them catching up to us. Leaving Baton Rouge, we were stopped by some busybody local constable. The tall tale Josephus came up with made me think he should be writing dime novels in New York instead of wasting his time as a church handyman.

The rain kept up the whole time, a hot feverish thing that had no deathly chill, no lingering shadow of pneumonia or typhus, just the dream-filled heat of Lucy beside me. When the wagon at last creaked to a stop, it was a day and a night and a day later in the town of Revenant on the East Texas border.

I was in a nightmarish half-sleep and, when Lucy gently shook me, I shot bolt upright out of the wagon in a convulsion of delirium. My wide-eyed expression, my ghostly pallor and rigid catatonic stare threw a good scare into her, and she looked at me aghast.

"Santo – "

I suddenly regained my senses and just as quickly crumpled to my knees. She sank down beside me. With Josephus' help, she somehow managed to get me on my feet – which was quite an achievement in the rain and mud – and then into the rundown adobe inn. Downstairs there was a little white-haired Indian woman with smiling eyes who, I guess, ran the place. She started laughing as soon as she saw them bring me in – I suppose she thought I was dead drunk – and didn't stop laughing until she saw how bad my left hand and arm was. Then she went sober, jabbering at Lucy in broken English about how her sister was married to a doctor and that she'd go out right away to fetch him. Just like that. No hesitation, no hemming nor hawing about leaving us there while she was gone. She trusted us right off, bless her soul. Coupled with me being at Death's door, it made me kind of misty-eyed, and I whispered a prayer that her kindness and innocence wouldn't one day help her to get her throat cut.

It didn't take her long to come back with the doctor, maybe ten minutes. And then they had me stretched out on the bar so he could take a good look at the damage.

He'd brought his wife with him, the old woman's sister, and surprisingly enough she proved an accomplished nurse, following his instructions to the letter. As a doctor, he was about as far removed from Marleybone as you cold get. There was a gentle fervor in his eyes that instilled confidence and hope the minute you looked into them.

I lay there, staring up at the wood ceiling. Everything was pretty much in shadows until the doctor brought over a kerosene lamp and gave it to his wife to hold above me.

Lucy came up on the other side of the doc and smiled at me.

"I'll be right back, honey. I'm going to pay Josephus and then let him go."

I tried to smile back at her and all at once realized how weak I was. It took a Herculean effort just to move my facial muscles. I heard her walking to the door where Josephus was waiting. She gave him a little money for both the wagon and his help, and told him he could take one of the horses. I didn't hear exactly what he answered at first because the doctor had started snipping away my shirtsleeve. When he had the cloth cut off, Josephus was still rambling on about how grateful he was, and how it hadn't been any trouble at all him helping us like he had, and asking her if she was sure she didn't want him to stick around a while longer. Then he was gone, and she was by my side again.

"I can hold that." She reached out to the doc's wife for the lamp.

"Go ahead, Maria. I'm going to need your help for other things."

It was the first time I'd heard him speak, and his grave tone of voice scared me. His wife handed the lamp over to Lucy.

"Son, I'm not going to kid around with you. This is bad. I'm afraid I'm going to have to take your arm off at the shoulder. If I don't, you haven't got a chance. The infection here in your hand is spreading like wildfire. And these stitches in your shoulder – well, maybe if you'd been able to rest and keep it cleaner and didn't have the gangrene setting in to your hand – but you see, if it spreads to your shoulder – "

He didn't have to draw me a picture.

"I get you," I whispered, "I figured as much already. Do what you have to."

He nodded grimly. His hands were long, slender and tapered like an artist's hands, and the graceful, tender way he moved them against my skin made me feel better. I tried to guess how old he was but couldn't. His grey hair and steely grey eyes looked to belong to a man who was at least in his sixties. But the taut, uncreased skin of his face and supple hands said different.

"Louisa, you'd better get him something to drink."

His white-haired sister-in-law handed him a glass and a bottle of rye, and he poured me a good four fingers of it.

"Here, son, you'd better take this. You're going to need it."

I took the glass, and he propped my head up to help me drink. I let it go down slow and even until I'd drained the last drop. It hit me like a hammer. Lucy had taken off her suede jacket and bunched it up into a pillow for me. She smoothed my perspiring brow with her free hand and brushed my hair out of my eyes as I lay back down.

I drank more rye during that next half-hour while the doc and his wife, Maria, made their preparations. They took their time about it, giving me as much leeway as possible so I'd get good and drunk.

Finally, they came to the point where they were ready to do the deed, and, for the first time since coming in the place, I felt like I was going to be sick. Oh, for Marleybone and his laudanum! I held on the best I could, reaching out my good hand to hold Lucy's. Right before I passed out, I heard Louisa, the white-haired woman who owned the place, refer to me as Lucy's husband. She was a crafty old bird and didn't miss a trick. I knew she had to have seen Lucy's wedding ring. I looked up to see Lucy's reaction to it, but she only stared down at me with her warm, limpid eyes. I'd expected her to deny it to the old woman. But no denial came. It was the last thing I remember happening that night.

23

I awoke the next afternoon out on the verandah. The rain had stopped and the sun was shining. A few pepper trees over the entranceway shaded me. A cool breeze whispering through the low-hanging branches, rustling the leaves, was the only sound.

I tried to move my head but couldn't. I was as weak as a kitten and felt a little feverish. From what I could see in front of me, it seemed that I was alone. And I didn't want to be. I wanted to see Lucy. I wanted to ask her why the doctor had decided not to cut off my arm.

Suddenly she was standing there before me, her hair washed and her face scrubbed, and wearing a simple white cotton peasant dress I'd never seen.

"Don't try to talk, darling. You're all right, but you've lost a lot of blood. The doctor had to have me give you a transfusion."

"But – " I was incredulous. How the hell had I lost the blood? I moved my head just a little to the left so I could watch my fingers as I flexed them. But they weren't there. There wasn't anything there anymore. How could it be? I could still feel my arm, my hand, my fingers. I could still feel the searing pain.

"The doctor told me you'd probably not be able to tell at first. It's something the rest of your body hasn't gotten used to yet."

I shut my eyes, trying to stifle a yell and wasn't completely successful. A half-strangled moan welled-up in my throat. And then she was there holding my head to her breast, whispering soothing words in my ear.

"It couldn't be helped. You know that, Santo." She looked me in the eye, and I grimaced. "The doctor said you should be fine in a couple of days. Right now, though, you need some rest."

"We…don't…have time." The words were a real effort.

"We can't worry about Charlie and my father. Not now. If you travel before you've regained your strength, it could be fatal."

So I lay there the rest of the day. When it got dark, Lucy and Louisa carted me inside to a cozy little room behind the kitchen. And the whole time it was eating away at me inside, wondering when they'd show up – if they ever would. Scared to death that they'd catch up to us while I was in a vulnerable position and couldn't lift a finger to fight back.

It didn't seem to bother Lucy, though. At least she wasn't letting on if it did.

We spent the next couple of days like that – Lucy and the old woman waiting on me hand and foot, nursing me back to health. On the third and final day there, the doctor came to see me again. I was able to walk short distances without tiring, and he was happy to see the progress I'd made. The infection was gone with the arm, and he assured me, despite the awkwardness I was experiencing, I was well on the road to recovery.

Awkwardness was an understatement. Having to get used to life with a significant part of me dead and buried was a grueling task. It wearied me just to think about it – let alone perform once simple chores with such a harrowing disadvantage. To his and Lucy's credit, they didn't cut me any slack. As soon as I gave any evidence of feeling sorry for myself, they were jumping all over me. After all, they were right. There was nothing to be done except to make the best of it. I was at a disadvantage, sure, but I'd always thrived on surmounting impossible odds. That's how Lucy'd put it, kind of half-joking about the terrible things we'd both been through together, the gauntlet we'd had to run. It was a good thing that she didn't let me get morose, refused to allow me to wallow in maudlin sentiment, or we would've never gotten away from Louisa's cantina. I don't know what I would've done if Lucy hadn't've been there to see me through it.

I said goodbye to the doc, and he wished us both well. Lucy followed him to his horse, and I could see her delving into the folds of her bodice, pulling out the money to pay him. He graciously accepted it and tipped his hat to her, bowed, then climbed on his horse. She waved at him as he galloped away.

I sat there in the shade on the verandah until it got dusk – just thinking, trying to figure out what lay ahead for us. Just as the moon rose and the stars came out, I heard Lucy in the kitchen, talking to Louisa about various things. Nothing really caught my ear at first. It was small talk, the old woman explaining why there weren't too many travelers through the region at that time of year – too many flash floods; how she was a brave and independent old soul and didn't much mind running the place all by her lonesome. She proudly confessed she wasn't afraid of anything and had, in fact, sent several desperadoes off to meet their maker in her time. As I was saying, nothing really caught my ear. Not until she brought up my being Lucy's husband again. Then something she must've seen in Lucy's face made her stop.

"Senora Brady? Am I wrong to call you by Senor Brady's name? Is he not your husband?"

There was a pause.

"No, Louisa, Senor Brady is not my husband."

"But you do love him?"

Lucy must've nodded because the old woman went on.

"Why don't you marry then?"

"I can't."

"Why not? That ring there on your finger – you are already married?"

She sure was a nosy old hen.

"Yes, in a way."

"I do not understand. What is this 'way' you speak of?"

There was silence for a few moments, then Louisa started up again.

"Senora, I tell you, I have seen many a couple that should never have come together. But you two children are not one of them. Everything about you and Senor Brady says you are husband and wife. The looks you give each other, the words you speak to each other. It is truly something that was meant to be. Planned out by God Himself."

"Do you think so?" There was an odd tone in Lucy's voice – it was something she wanted to believe. Even though I was all alone out there on the verandah, it made me blush.

"Si. But I tell you – " Louisa faltered, then continued on, figuring out as she went along what to say to convince Lucy.

"Have you ever heard of something called The Wedding Dice?"

"No, I haven't."

"Well, The Wedding Dice is an old custom in the province of Mexico where I was born." I could hear Louisa moving around there in the kitchen, opening drawers and cupboards as if she was looking for something. "Ah, here they are." There was a glowing warmth of satisfaction in her voice. "These dice are not like regular dice."

"They're so big. And they have pictures painted all over them."

"This die is for the man, this one for the woman. The pictures you see on them are of the different duties and responsibilities each person has in their lifetime. Those of the man, those of the woman. If the dice are thrown and matching pictures come up, then it is in the stars that a couple should be married. The legend says it is God's will. Here..."

Lucy must have taken them from her. "Bueno." The old woman was ecstatic.

"What do I do?"

"Take them in both hands... si, that is right, my dear... now, shake them..."

I could hear her rattling them, the two pieces banging together.

"Close your eyes and ask our Lord for guidance..."

Lucy let go of them, and they crashed against something metallic. There was a moment of silence.

"You see, it is meant to be."

I went inside about half an hour later when they called me for supper. Louisa was aglow with what she thought to be her and Lucy's little secret. I didn't let on that I'd heard anything. Slowly, relishing each bite, I ate the meal. There wasn't much talk amongst us, just a kind of comfortable tension. I could really see it in Lucy. She didn't seem to have much of an appetite and kept blushing every time I looked at her.

"What's wrong, honey?"

She fidgeted, and Louisa giggled and started to clear the table.

"You haven't been able to sit still all through supper."

She gave me a nervous half-smile, not sure what to say, folded her hands on the table until her knuckles turned white, then shyly lowered her head to stare down at them.

"Santo, the last day or two's been the first time I've had to really rest in I don't know how long. You know, just sit and think – "

"Yeah?"

"Well, I don't know why, but I haven't been too worried about

Charlie and the old bastard. I haven't been thinking about them."

"What have you been thinking about, then?"

She shrugged, stopped herself, wiped away the perspiration that had gathered on her upper lip with the back of her hand and laughed.

"You."

The old woman shuffled quickly out of the room.

"Yes?"

She nodded and propped her chin on one hand, staring at me.

"Well, do you know what I've been thinking about all day?" I asked.

She started to get a little worried at that. I could've hugged her to death, she looked so anxious and forlorn.

"No – "

"I've been thinking about you." I smiled at her, and she let out a sigh of relief. She slowly sent her hands out to touch mine. "That we should get married."

Confused, she shook her head, speechless.

"All this, what we have between us, is tearing you apart. Isn't that right?"

She nodded. "The vows I took when I was in the convent – well, I'd be lying if I was to say there wasn't a part of me that meant them."

"And the part of you that had doubts?"

"My father and stepmother did their best to pretend that part didn't exist. They knew that I was scared. They didn't care about my feelings, though. They just talked and talked and talked at me until they were blue in the face. Finally, I was so damn weak, I gave in, I took my vows. And I've never felt right about breaking them. No matter how it came about that I took them. But – and this is a mighty big 'but' – I love you, Santo. Completely, in every way. There isn't a power on Earth that could convince me that our love for each other is wrong."

"I feel the same way about you."

A tear rolled down her cheek as I said it, and she clutched at my hand again.

24

We left the next morning just before dawn. Louisa kissed the both of us
and handed us a basket of food. She'd already sold Lucy a second horse
to hitch up to the wagon and had prepared a makeshift mattress in the
back – flour and corn meal sacks stuffed with leaves – so that when
I became tired I could rest without us having to stop. She warned
us again about the flash floods that had been occurring, especially
farther west. The amount of rainfall had been exorbitant for the time
of year, and the flat countryside was dangerous in the event of a violent
downpour. We thanked her and headed out, traveling in a southwesterly
direction.

We weren't exactly sure where we were going. We'd talked a
bit and had come up with a vague idea of buying a few acres of land
somewhere along the way with the rest of our money. I suppose it was a
naïve idea, but we were both sick of the aimless wandering – we'd been
doing it too long and knew it for the emotion-killing thing that it was.
What we would do with the land once we had it in our possession was
another story. I don't think we'd really thought it out that far. I suppose
there'd been some general idea about farming and raising a few head
of cattle. Nothing too ambitious, but something that could sustain us as
a hardworking family over the years ahead. And family was what we
wanted to be. She was all the family I had left in the world, and she felt

the same way about me.

We traveled for four days straight without seeing a soul. The weather was hot and damp, the sky perpetually overcast, but nothing particularly inclement befell us.

When we finally made the decision to stop, it was a random choice, a very small village near where the Little River branches off from the Brazos – some miles southeast of Waco. The population of one hundred or so Indian and Mexican dirt farmers was sparsely settled over an area of rolling hills and arid flatland. The pathetic main street was a half block long consisting of a cantina, a livery stable, a general store, an ancient rooming house and a crumbling adobe church.

Why we stopped there was a mystery to me. Maybe because we were at last running low on food and water. But the place, too, seemed to offer a small measure of tranquility. You could tell immediately that the citizens were a gentle, easygoing people. Despite the obvious poverty, the harsh, backbreaking life of trying to extract a simple existence from a barely fertile territory, they seemed to possess a hearty sense of humor and a surprising concern for each other's welfare. You could see it in their haggard, yet determined faces, in their warm friendly eyes. Life was hard, damn near impossible at times, but cynicism hadn't taken any foothold there.

We came into town about noon and stopped at the church first thing. Lucy wanted to, for some strange reason, so we tied up the horses and went inside. It was dark and musty-smelling, and when the rotting doors closed behind us, you couldn't see your hand in front of your face. Gradually, my eyes became used to the dim light, and I saw that there were two candles burning at the far end on either side of the altar. I sat down in the last pew while Lucy walked to the front, kneeling reverently on the dusty dirt floor. She made the sign of the cross, placed her hands together pointing heavenwards in an attitude of prayer, and stared up into the face of a gigantic stone Christ hanging from one of the biggest crosses I'd ever seen.

Whatever feelings about God I do have, prayer in a man-made church has never been amongst them.

Just as Lucy stood to leave, a door opened a few yards beyond her, and an elderly priest dressed in a long brown robe appeared from the shadows.

"Hello, my child. You are a stranger to me. Can I be of assistance to you?"

Lucy backed up a few steps, throwing a glance over her shoulder at me. I shakily stood – as I was still fairly weak – and started down the aisle.

"Do not be afraid. No one will harm you here."

"I'm sure they won't."

He looked startled at the sound of my voice, as he hadn't seen me. But he quickly regained his composure.

I came up behind Lucy and put my arm around her shoulder in a protective gesture.

"You two look like you've been traveling for days."

"We have been. We'd like to find a place to rest."

Lucy chimed in, still nervous. "We'd also like to find someone to marry us."

His bushy white eyebrows arched, and he gave us a bemused smile. "I see. Well, I'm sure you must know that I could perform the ceremony for you. If you'd like me to."

Lucy twisted her head round again to see what I thought about the idea. I shook my head, amused at her determination, then nodded. Her face lit up.

"Would you like to have a meal first and get cleaned up?"

"Let's do it right away."

"Are either of you Catholic?"

I felt Lucy stiffen at the question. She hesitated for a few seconds, then answered. "I am, Father."

"Well, then, would you like me to hear your confession first?"

I could tell she was frightened, but she went right ahead anyway and nodded.

He turned, folding his hands together in the enormous sleeves of his robe. She followed him over to a twin-closet structure off to one side of the pews, and I watched them with puzzlement. I still wasn't sure what the strange rite was all about but had the feeling it was going to take some time, so I sat down to wait.

As it turned out, the padre was a pretty understanding fellow. Later Lucy told me how she'd related the whole story of her being in the convent to him. He released her from her vows as she'd been coerced into taking them and absolved her from her sins – an idea, for the life of me, I can't take to, let alone understand. But it made her happy. When she came out of the confessional, her face was beaming, and tears streamed down her face from all the pent-up emotion that had finally been released.

The padre married us there in the candlelight. And when we left the church together, we left as husband and wife.

25

The one-armed bit hit me again a lot harder after we'd been there for a few days. We'd bought a little place a couple of miles outside of town – a ramshackle three room cabin lying at the foot of a hill in the bottomlands about a quarter of a mile west of the Brazos River. The owner, who also had the general store in town, had needed cash and given us a reasonable price. The land was probably a bit more fertile than some of the other farms in the area due to its proximity to the water. In fact, the whole oblong tract had once been riverbottom nearly a decade before. A dam had been built a quarter of a mile away from us on our other side. It had reduced and diverted a fair size of tributary of the Brazos to no more than a gentle stream coursing through our property down into town. I hadn't gone to look at the dam yet but imagined it to be a staggeringly profound engineering feat for the people in the area – considering the tools they'd had to work with.

There was a low shed and a broken down pen set about thirty yards from the house, and Lucy and I had lofty plans for turning them into a barn and corral.

I suppose it must've been the isolation as much as anything else, but I suddenly came down with such a fit of depression it was all I could do to stop myself from putting the Peacemaker barrel to my mouth and pulling the trigger. It lasted a good week and, even though

Lucy was worried out of her mind, she left me alone – at least at first. When she saw I wasn't coming out of it after the first day or two, that I wasn't eating and couldn't get a wink of sleep, she gave me a good talking to. It didn't do any good. I felt dead, inside and out, a dry husk, and I was oblivious to the fact that she saw me as a hell of a lot more than just a pathetic shell of a man.

It was on one of those moonless, sleepless nights that I snapped out of it. I'd been lying there in the dark, gazing out the open window at the millions of stars, when I got a sudden urge to look over at Lucy sleeping peacefully beside me. Something about the way she lay there so vulnerable in slumber, in such an unconscious attitude of trust, overwhelmed me, and I finally got enough outside myself to remember my responsibility to not only her but myself.

After all, I'd still be able to build things, make love, shoot a gun – even though a part of me was missing. It'd take a hell of a lot of getting used to, but that was just too bad. It was my lot in life, and to do anything else besides let the chips fall where they may was futile. It was the second time since I'd lost my arm that it had hit me that way, and I wondered how many more times I'd have to go through the self-inflicted torture and self-doubt before I would fully come to terms with it.

Needless to say, after relieving old man Damien of his daughter's ransom, a ransom he'd never intended to pay, we were pretty comfortable. Even after buying the place, we had a healthy chunk of the money left.

It was a hot, muggy morning with the air hanging still that I rode the buckboard into town to see about buying a couple of cows that a good friend of the priest, Father Mendoza, had to sell. Before going over to the church where I was to meet the man, I stopped in at the cantina for a beer. It hadn't been that long a ride, but the hours I'd put in earlier with Lucy repairing the corral had helped me work up a powerful thirst.

The cantina was a large, low-ceilinged place consisting of two big rooms for eating, drinking and dancing, a kitchen and a small room in the back that served as living quarters for the owner and his wife. Compared to Louisa's place, it was a luxurious nightspot. But that still wasn't saying much. They kept it dark in there during the day, and it usually took a good five or six minutes for your eyes to adjust.

I picked a small table in one corner well away from the door and settled down to relax in a high-backed chair. I'd been there maybe ten minutes and was about halfway through my beer, when I heard him come in.

I knew right away who it was. And despite his bumbling ineptitude, his presence there sent a chill up my spine. I knew it had to have been an accident him stumbling in there like that. It couldn't have been anything else. But the very fact he was there told me they were still looking for us. If he started asking about Lucy – it seemed in the few weeks we'd been there we'd already made a lot of friends, and I was hoping that whoever was asked would have the brains to put two and two together and not go blabbing to a total stranger.

Marleybone was downright quiet at first, which, considering his big mouth, was fairly unusual. All he'd asked for was a glass of mescal. I sat stock still with my back to him, sipped my beer and waited for what was going to happen next. I didn't have long to wait.

There was the jingle of spurs coming into the place and a long, heavy stride.

"Goddamn it, you useless relic. You have to get a sloppy drunk everywhere you go?"

It was Charlie.

"Your father has a great deal more respect for my position. He has the good sense to recognize my standing in the medical community and realize my invaluable worth on a trek such as this."

"Shut your foul-smelling trap!"

Things hadn't changed much. I wondered why old man Damien had brought Marleybone along.

Charlie ordered a shot of rye, downed it, then began harping on Marleybone again.

"Listen, you son-of-a-bitch. You want to stick with us, finish that cactus pisswater or we'll leave you here and take your horse with us. Pa's got a damn good idea where they are."

Marleybone harrumphed indignantly, tossed the rest of it down, then let Charlie drag him out into the blinding sunlight.

As soon as I heard the stamping of hooves, I jumped up and ran to the door. They were headed up over the hill, back towards our place.

26

I told the owner of the cantina, an Irish-Mex fellow named Jaimie, what the score was and that there might be trouble. I knew right off he didn't want to get involved. He promised me he'd have his son ride for the county sheriff. But the sheriff was at least one good day's ride.

I unhitched one of the horses, slapped a blanket over it and left the wagon tied up in Jaimie's care. By the time I reached the top of the rise overlooking our place, everything was quiet. There weren't any horses tethered anywhere in sight. Old man Damien was a pretty slick character. I knew that once he'd found me absent from the place, he'd do everything in his power to make things appear normal. All the better to make certain I returned unsuspecting and unawares.

I pulled the horse back down the hill and tied her to the branch of a scrub oak. Then I carefully made my way up, drawing my gun and getting on all fours as I reached the top.

It was deathly quiet. The old man was wrong to make things so quiet. An idiot tinhorn farmboy would've known something was up. But I didn't tip my hand. I just lay there patiently and waited.

The minutes ticked by in my head. I'm not sure how long it really was that I waited there. Maybe two or three hours. After the first hour, it started getting to me. There wasn't any shade where I was so I was sweating like all get out. To make matters worse, big Mexican horseflies kept trying to land on me. But I kept waiting. Waiting for something to happen. Waiting for a sound, anything that would give me an excuse to blow all their brains out. Of course, the trick would be to blow their brains out first, before they could blow out mine.

When I'd seen them silhouetted against the sun, cresting the hill back near the cantina, it looked like there was only one other besides the old man, Charlie, and Marleybone. Discounting the old man and Marleybone, that evened the odds a little. On the other hand, I hadn't fired the gun since my arm had come off, let alone practiced with it. I knew that despite my generally good reflexes, there would still be a balance problem in the way I held myself.

During the second hour, that notion joined the flies in eating away at me. Towards the end, I had to fight dropping off to sleep. The sweltering sun and the muggy closeness of the air was a potent draught for drowsiness.

Then, all of a sudden it came. A voice – her voice cutting through the heat. She sounded calm, reserved.

"You'll never get him, Charlie."

"Shut up."

"You won't. He's smarter than all of you put together." Christ! It was like she was right there next to me.

I heard him slap her as answer, and the thwack sound his hand made hitting her face made me tremble with rage.

"Charles, we don't need any of that. You can save it for him when he gets back." Old man Damien – always thinking of me. His craggy, quavery voice was as clear as a bell. I marveled at the way the sound carried across the hundred or so yards between us.

"Mr. Damien?" It was a new voice. A strong, yet polite voice.

"Yes, Mr. Corey?"

"If you'll permit me, I'm actually quite concerned about the fact that you've placed all of our horses out of our own sight as well as Brady's." An educated voice.

"That's right, Pa. And Marleybone guarding them."

The old man coughed before he answered, then gave his explanation. His tone was condescending and somewhat petulant, like he was explaining a very simple problem in arithmetic to a schoolhouse full of thick-headed children.

"Mr. Corey, I'm surprised at you. Logic tells us that Brady will approach from the direction of town. There's no need for concern because he'll never come near those hills on our other side." So that was it.

"Unless he hears you filibustering it all over creation."

"Charles!"

"Don't you 'Charles' me. I don't like this. He should've been back hours ago. At least to hear her tell it after we whipped it out of her. He could be anywhere out there. He could be right outside that window listening to our every word."

"Son, your point it well taken. Now, will you kindly shut your mouth!"

There was the sound of breaking glass – Charlie losing his temper and blowing off steam I suppose – then silence again.

I made sure the mare was tied nice and secure, then started circling around the base of the low hills, working my way in the direction of where the horses would be. There was only one point on the route where I could possibly be spotted from the house, and I didn't think it too likely, considering the angle and the dense weeds spanning the entire twenty yards.

When I came to the weeds, I sank down on my belly and crawled like a snake. The idea of a snake made me think of the nest of rattlers I'd found in the shed when we'd first moved in. We'd had a devil of a time getting rid of them because of what else was in the shed. I guess at one point the previous owner had had ambitions to strike it rich. He'd mentioned something about being a miner in his younger days before settling down and building his general store. But he hadn't mentioned the boxes of dynamite he'd left stacked haphazardly in that old lean-to. Because of the stuff, we hadn't been ale to shoot the snakes. And we hadn't been able to chase them out into the open, either. Trying that only made them slither deeper into the cache of explosives. We had had to wrap several layers of burlap around our arms and legs, then cautiously employ a pitchfork and shovel as our tools of extermination. It had worked for the most part, but a couple of them had streaked out of the shed into the brush. I prayed I wouldn't run into one of them right then.

It took me a while, what with the one arm. It probably wasn't more than half an hour, but at the time it seemed like years that I was creeping through those weeds. Fear for Lucy's life overcame fear for myself. I really was goddamned scared. I was scared of them letting their patience wear thin, coming out all of a sudden and stumbling over me. I was scared of two inch fangs dripping with poison sinking into my face.

At last, I came to the shrub-covered bend beyond which lay Marleybone and the horses. True to his character, Marleybone guarded the mounts in his charge with his customary rigor – sprawled horizontally, his top hat shading his face and snoring loud enough of wake the dead.

I did my best to avoid trampling the dry, brittle debris from several dead mesquite trees. I untied the four horses from a scrawny scrub. When I slapped them on their rears and sent them galloping upstream over the rise towards the dam at the Brazos, Marleybone gave a snort. He twitched spasmodically in sleep and brushed away the herd of flies congregating on his filthy hat. I drew the Peacemaker, dropped quietly down on my knees beside him, then noisily cocked the hammer. He sprung to a sitting position, and his hat tumbled into his lap. The sun was behind me, so he had to squint and shade his eyes to get a good look.

"Hello, Doc. Nice to see you."

He scrambled to his feet and put up his shaking hands in an attitude of surrender.

"Now, Brady, my good fellow, don't lose your head."

I gave him a devilish grin, "Why not, Doc? I've already lost an arm."

"That was not my doing, sir. You'll recall that at one point I dressed said departed appendage. And did one bang-up job, I might add."

"Considering you were as drunk as a skunk."

"If I hadn't had the drink, my poor palsied hands, arthritically crippled as they are, would've been useless to you."

I moved behind him and nudged him with the gun. "C'mon, we're going to pay a visit to your employer."

"Yes, yes, that's correct, Mr. Brady. I am, after all, only a hired hand. So to speak. And they are certainly more culpable in regards to your loss of limb than I."

"At least we agree on something."

"There is s-s-something – " he stammered, unsure of himself, debating the wisdom of what he was going to tell me. "Mr. Damien's son, Charlie, has gone completely mad. I suppose you know that?" I stared at him, unblinking, as he went on. "Ever since you shot him in his hand, he's been totally unmanageable. Mr. Damien hired this other fellow, Mr. Corey, to keep Charles in line as much to help find you two. Charles… murdered an old woman a few days back."

A vision of Louisa bidding us farewell jumped into my mind.

"What old woman?"

"I don't know her name. S-S-She owned a small cantina near the East Texas border."

I looked grimly down at the ground.

"Mr. Damien was extremely upset and confided in me that – " He gave out with a raspy cough.

"Confided what?"

"That he was thinking of turning back, giving up this ridiculous expedition, this foolish crusade. B-but-but Charles wouldn't let him."

"I see."

His eyes lit up. "One thing I do remember about the old woman… she had in her possession a pair of children's blocks with the most marvelous pictures painted on them."

"That bastard. And what were you doing while Charlie shot her down?" I gave him a crack on the face with the gun butt.

"Aaarrhh!" He put both hands to his bleeding cheek and began to sob.

"Drinking up rotgut liquor that didn't even belong to you?!"

He fell to his knees, crying as much from shame as from the wound. I roughly yanked him up and kicked him in the ass. "Get going."

Before we rounded the hill that put us behind the house, I used my little finger to snag the collar of his sweat-stained coat. "Wait a minute."

I pushed him down on his knees with the gun, then crouching close to the ground, crept a couple more yards. I peered above a sun-baked juniper and could see the shed between us and the house. It was deathly quiet again, and no one was in sight. I motioned Marleybone with the gun, putting him back in front of me as a shield. When we came to the shed, I made him pause.

"Listen to me, Doctor, and listen good. Because your very life depends on what I'm going to tell you."

His mouth quivered – partly from fear, partly from alcoholic stupor. He cocked his head to hear my whispering.

"We're walking straight to the front door, keeping the shed between us as long as we can. When we get to the house, we stay glued to the wall away from the windows until we reach the door. Do you understand?"

He nodded.

"If you feel the slightest pressure of this gun barrel on your neck, you stop, understand?"

He nodded again, eager to please.

"Let's go."

I peeked around the corner that was angled away from the front room's window, then gave him a shove. We made the distance of five yards in record time. I kept looking around, both in front of and behind us, determined not to be surprised by Charlie. I thought of kicking the door in and surprising them but thought of Charlie again and decided against it.

I whispered in Marleybone's ear. "Knock."

He did as I told him. There was an awkward silence.

"Who – who is it?" It was Lucy's frightened voice.

"It is I, Doctor Marleybone."

Immediately, the door was thrown back, and the man called Corey thrust his angry face up next to Marleybone's.

"What the hell are you doing back – " He stopped as he saw me, sweeping a long greasy lock of white hair out of his face.

"Howdy." I used the gun to tip back my hat, grinned and aimed it at Corey over Marleybone's shoulder. I chuckled softly at his meticulous appearance – the manicured beard, the well-trimmed moustache, the velvet clothes of a dandyish gambler. He stepped backwards, genuinely surprised at seeing me. Charlie, with barely controlled rage, clenched and unclenched his left hand. Lucy let out a sigh of relief and began weeping. The old man was the only one who kept some degree of composure.

"At last, Mr. Brady. We've been waiting for you."

"So I see."

"Yes, we expected you quite some time ago."

"And I would've been here quite some time ago if I hadn't overheard the good doctor and your murdering butcher of a son back at the cantina."

Charlie bristled at my understated description of his character. The old man stepped between us before he could draw his gun.

"Charles, will you please try to control your temper?"

Wrinkling his brow, Charlie shot a puzzled stare at the old man, then looked at me. The old man turned.

"I don't understand you, Mr. Brady. What do you expect to gain from this?"

"My wife."

"What?" They all glanced at Lucy and back at me in unison. It was pretty damn funny.

"We were married at the church in town a few weeks ago. Just days after I had my arm amputated – an operation that would not have been necessary if it hadn't been for the friendly, loving treatment I received from my pal, Charlie."

"It's too bad they didn't cut out your eyes. You had it coming to
you."

I smiled at Charlie's poisonous behavior.

"'You had it coming to you' – is that what you said to the old
woman Louisa when you shot her to death?"

Lucy looked at me in shock. And Charlie locked his stare on
Marleybone, the fire growing wilder in his eyes.

"I didn't tell him anything, Charlie. I swear to—"

Charlie was too quick. The old man couldn't stop him. Before
I could draw a bead or Marleybone could finish his sentence, Charlie
pointed his gun at the good doctor's head and fired. The back of
Marleybone's skull exploded, and the flying blood blinded me. Lucy
screamed.

I don't know exactly what happened next – probably the
old man knocked Charlie's arm, because when the gun went off again,
the bullet smashed through the tin roof. Corey jumped across
Marelybone's corpse, grabbed my gun out of my hand and slugged
me across the face with it. I went down on my knees, falling over
Marleybone's outstretched dead arm. I tried to keep from passing out
as I wiped the blood out of my eyes.

"You damn fool." The old man's voice cracked. When I could
see again, the old man, livid with rage, was slapping Charlie with one
hand and taking away his pistol with the other. "You call yourself a son
of mine!"

Corey shook his head, obviously disgusted with the whole
situation. He bent down, grabbed Marleybone's arms and dragged the
body out of the way into a corner.

Satisfied that he had Charlie subdued, the old man came and
stood over me.

"And you, you filthy piece of poor white trash. My daughter is
no more married to you than she is to poor dead Marleybone there."

I gritted my teeth, giving him a nasty grin.

"You don't have a thing to smile about, Mr. Brady. I'm taking
Lucille back with me to St. Louis. And Mr. Corey here, who is a very
accomplished bounty hunter, will be returning you to the authorities
in New Orleans to stand trial for the murder of Dannahy, Jennings and
Moreau."

Meanwhile, Charlie had ripped the front window's flimsy linen
curtains off their rods and was staring out into the yard.

"Where's the wagon? We found wagon tracks leading both to

and away from here."

I got an idea and decided to tell the truth.

"I left it in town at the cantina."

The old man went over to Charlie and put a hand on his shoulder. "Charles, why don't you go and gather up the horses? Then we can leave Mr. Corey to tend to them while the two of us go into town to fetch the wagon. How would that be?"

Charlie didn't say a word nor move a muscle.

"It'd be much more comfortable traveling to Austin that way than in the saddle, don't you agree, son?"

Charlie hesitated, but I knew the old man had gotten through to him.

"Okay, Pa." He didn't look at any of us as he left the cabin and slammed the door.

"Austin?"

The old man gave me a condescending look.

"Yes, Mr. Brady. Charles, Lucille and I shall be taking a train from Austin to St. Louis. You didn't think I was contemplating a journey all the way to Missouri in a buckboard, did you?"

27

Corey and the old man didn't have enough rope to do the job properly, so they had to settle for tying Lucy's arms together, then my one arm to hers. The old man cursed at Corey, who was all thumbs. Gamblers aren't used to manual labor, I suppose. Or maybe the old man was losing his temper because of the cologne Corey was drenched with – to mask the fact he hadn't bathed in over a year.

It wasn't long before Charlie returned and, as usual, he was fit to be tied himself. He nearly took the door off its hinges as he stormed into the cabin.

"The goddamn horses aren't there!"

"What?" Corey and the old man were getting to be a regular Greek Chorus.

"Either that dumb, drunk son-of-a-bitch, Marleybone, didn't have them tied up, or this bastard – " he lunged at me so that Corey had to restrain him, " – this bastard let them loose. I could only find one over by that dam. Then I found what must be Brady's horse tied up over the other hill."

"Calm down, Charles. Two horses are sufficient for us to get to town. We can pick up another one while we're there." Then the old man turned to face me. "That was very foolish, Mr. Brady. You are only prolonging the agony."

He took hold of Charlie's arm, and they left.

I looked over at Lucy. She had her head bowed down so her hair hid her features.

Her body was wracked with misery and despair, her spirit crushed in defeat. When she at last felt my eyes on her, she raised her head. I bent sideways, brushing my mouth against hers, and she returned my kiss. A tear ran down along her nose so it fell on my upper lip. I tasted the warm, salty wetness of it. Corey turned his back for a moment, and I whispered in her ear.

"Don't give up, honey. We're not beaten as long as there's a breath left inside of me."

"All right, you two, break it up."

He positioned a chair on the other end of the room and sat down facing us. His long-barreled Colt rested in his lap.

"Do you know, Miss, why your brother hates you so much?"

Lucy's eyes became icy cold.

"Well, do you? For the same reason he hates himself. You've both got a lot of Indian blood in you."

"Why don't you shut up."

He didn't pay any attention to me, just kept on going. "That's right. You're not quite a half-breed, but even a quarter Blackfoot's a lot of Indian. He thinks that's why you stopped being a nun and became a whore." He laughed. "Thinks the same thing about himself. He's so crazy, we've been having to keep him away from liquor all the way from New Orleans. Can't hold his drink at all." He flashed his pearly white teeth in a hideous smile. "Too bad. Especially for the old man. Just think of it – to have offspring like you two."

He was getting to Lucy, and she violently shook her head with frustration.

"You bastard. Shut your goddamn dirty mouth." My voice was hoarse with anger.

His laughter echoed in the room. "You should've seen him when we were in that greaser's excuse for a town. If your father and me hadn't had him on a short leash, he would've burnt down the whole village looking for you."

After that he didn't say anything more. The three of us just sat there in silence, waiting. When it got to be about a half an hour since they'd left, he started to have trouble keeping his head up. A couple more minutes, and he was slumped in the chair, snoring.

I started working on the ropes with my hand, trying to squirm loose, all the time listening as hard as I could for their return.

My eyes wandered around the room while I struggled, and the brace of wall to my left caught my attention. The wooden planks didn't come flush to the floor for a space of two or three inches along five feet of the bottom, so there was a narrow open place to the outside. I'd meant to fix it several days before but had never gotten around to it. Not only did it let in a draft at night, but there was enough room for all manner of scorpions, snakes and spiders to creep through into the house. Especially that time of day when the blistering sun favored that side. As if it had read my mind, a squat, blunt-nosed reptilian face peered beneath the crack. It was the head of a sidewinder, like the ones from the shed. He kept spitting his tongue in and out, testing the safety and temperature of the cooler place. It cautiously slithered into the room.

Lucy gasped when she saw it.

"Don't panic, honey. We're going to get that little fellow to work for us."

She gulped as the snake slid beneath the rusty, cast iron stove behind Corey. It brushed against something under there, and a piece of charcoal clunked onto the floor from the bottom grating. Corey sprang awake, his gun aimed as steady as a rock at the both of us. He wiped at his eyes with a balled-up fist, then whirled around to the stove. A dry rustling was coming out of it. He flexed his knees, crouching on the floor, and cocked the gun.

I looked over at Lucy and saw her eyes closed and her lips moving soundlessly in prayer. When I turned back, I saw that Corey had his free hand on the oven door. All of a sudden, he yanked it open. Before he could fire, the snake struck him in the face. The gun flew out of his hand, and he yelled, filled with shock and horrible pain. The snake fell free of him and coiled itself under the chair. Corey didn't even notice. Both hands were pressed against his left cheek – it was trickling a stream of blood and already beginning to swell. He hit the door like he'd been shot from a cannon, tearing it off its hinges – the whole time wailing unintelligible words – then disappeared into the yard. After five minutes or so, it was quiet, and I knew he must be either dying or dead.

Lucy had her eyes riveted on the snake.

"Santo, we've got to get loose from these ropes."

I nodded, struggling frantically against the nerve-numbing tightness of the knots. I thought of us both getting to our feet and simply walking out, then realized that Cory had tied Lucy's ankles together.

Gradually, the ropes were loosening. But our progress was so slow. I was scared to death that the snake or Charlie or both would get to us before we were free. Lucy was unconsciously grinding her teeth with panicked determination, and I knew she felt the same way.

"Santo, I'm scared. I'm scared we're not going to get out of this alive."

"Don't think like that. We make our own luck, honey. Any minute now – "

"I know. We've been making our own luck right along. That's the trouble – it's all been bad."

Then the snake started to move. I don't know what set him off. Maybe the sound of our voices. Maybe the waves of frightened heat it felt coming off our bodies. I knew that snakes could sense fear, and there was enough of it between the two of us to rile up a whole roomful of rattlers. It was about three feet away when we finally got ourselves free. Right then Charlie banged through the open door. We both had been so distracted neither of us had heard them ride up. The rattler froze. Charlie looked at it dumbly and clumsily drew his pistol. When the old man came in the room, the rattling started. Charlie fired at it and missed just as it sprang. He was too late to keep it from burying its head in Lucy's stomach. All three of us – Lucy, Charlie and me – began screaming at once. I yanked the snake by its tail and, as it came free, its stubborn fangs pulled away bloody shreds of Lucy's flesh. In one quick motion, I slammed the thing down on the floor as hard as I could, and its head popped.

Lucy was turning white, already shivering with convulsions. I tore away the ripped cloth and pressed my mouth down on the gaping wound, sucked poisoned blood, spit it out, sucked, spit it out, sucked, spit it out – over and over again.

"Santo. I don't want to die. I don't want to die like this!" She crossed herself while reaching out to me with her other palsied hand. Her breath was coming in shuddering gasps, and I could tell that her lungs were freezing up on her. The snake must've released a huge dose of venom. I hadn't sucked enough of the stuff out. It had gone into her system too close to her heart.

Tears stung my eyes and blurred my vision. I was losing the one woman I'd ever really loved. I was losing my wife. She was dying before my very eyes, and I was powerless to lift a finger to help her. I couldn't even take away the terrifying spasms of pain that wracked her whole body.

Her lids fluttered, her eyes rolled back into her head, and she spoke her last words to me – "I – " then died with a rattling gasp. I held onto her hand until my knuckles went white and buried my face in her breast.

Someone spoke behind me. I raised my head and saw Charlie standing over us.

"You did this to her."

He'd been standing paralyzed with fear while his sister died an agonizing death. But when he'd come out of it, he'd immediately looked for someone to blame. I was the obvious choice.

I let go of Lucy's hand and shut her eyes.

Deep in shock, the old man was sitting stock-still in the chair and staring into space.

"You did this to her!"

I looked back up at Charlie just as he brought the gun butt down on my face.

28

When I came to, I was lying in the doorway to the place. My right eye was swollen shut, but I could make out the old man carrying Lucy to the buckboard. He reverently laid her out on the wagon bed. The horse that was hitched up had a garish streak of blood running down its flank – Charlie had been playing with his bullwhip again. I looked around the yard, but he was nowhere in sight.

I tried to stand up, but couldn't – my head was pounding too much. It felt like the clapper inside some gigantic cathedral bell.

Suddenly it hit me that Lucy was gone for good, and I'd never see her alive again. Everything that had happened to us since we'd met felt like a dream. It was gone. It was over. And I was totally, completely alone.

There was someone rooting around in the shed. I tried to figure out who it was, then realized that Charlie, the old man and me were the only ones left. So it had to be Charlie.

I shakily got to my feet.

The old man was in more of a trance than I was. When I came up to the wagon and looked down at Lucy's lifeless body, he just stood there, staring off into the distance.

The stupid bastards. If they'd only left us alone, she'd still be alive. I had to control an urge to pick up a rock and smash in the old man's head. But what was the use? It wouldn't bring Lucy back.

I ambled unsteadily towards the shed.

The door was open. Charlie suddenly burst out, his big hands wrapped around an armful of dynamite. He brushed me aside, and, without looking, stepped over Corey's bloated corpse that lay in the middle of the yard. He made a beeline to one of the free horses, then deposited the dynamite in the saddlebags. I was in too much of a stupor to figure out what he was doing. Not until he climbed into the saddle, slapped his whip, and spurred the horse in the direction of the dam. Even then I thought, "No, he couldn't be that crazy." Blowing up the dam wouldn't help. He'd just wipe out a town full of innocent people, poor Indian dirt farmers, kill himself and his old man as well, in the process. Then Corey's idle chatter came back to me. How Charlie would've gladly burned down the village. How he passionately hated the Indian blood inside Lucy, inside himself.

The old man was fumbling with the other free horse, trying to get it into the double harness attached to the wagon. I grabbed the antique Dragoon pistol he had tucked in his waistband, then pushed him away. He lost his balance and landed on his ass in a cloud of dust. As I jumped on the horse to race after Charlie, I glanced over my shoulder and saw him still sitting there, not even looking after me.

When I reached the dam, Charlie was already prancing along the top, balancing himself precariously like he was walking a circus tightrope. I thought of picking him off right from where I was – but, what with my screwed-up eye, I was afraid of hitting the bundle of dynamite cradled in his arms.

He stopped in the center and began placing the sticks together in a clump. The dam seemed pretty solid, but I knew it could never withstand the kind of blast Charlie had planned. Brick, mortar, mud, huge timbers – you name it – whatever the people had been able to come up with to block the overflow of the Brazos was packed tight in one huge mass.

I leapt from the horse and scrambled up the rise that led to the nearest side, splashing my way through the knee-deep stream that coursed from a carefully burrowed duct near the top.

Charlie was so wrapped up in his crazy scheme, he hadn't seen me yet. I saw that he'd lit a cigar and could light off a fuse at the slightest provocation. The way he was acting had me convinced he didn't give a good goddamn whether he lived or died.

I kept having to fight the notion to just run back to my horse and get the hell out of there. It was a hundred to one chance I'd be able to stop him before he set off a charge. The way I felt, though, it didn't matter – I had nothing to lose. Lucy was gone.

He raised his head, anxiously surveying the waters that snaked off into the distance. There'd been a lot of rain in that last month, and the river was gorged to the bursting point. He smiled, removing the cigar from his mouth, licking his lips. That's when he saw me. Without hesitation, he pressed the burning ember to a fuse, and it sparked.

I shook my head, aimed the gun and fired, hitting him right between the eyes. He toppled into the water.

I knew I'd never be able to reach the fuse in time, so turned tail and scurried back down the hill to my horse. I twisted around as I ran – that's when it went off and all hell broke loose.

A piece of rock smashed into me, and I blacked out.

When I came to I was being buffeted in the raging, foaming tide from the unleashed river. I kept going under, bobbing up and down, struggling with all my might, kicking with my last bit of strength to reach the surface again. It was quickly becoming a monotonous, exhausting routine. Until I caught sight of the house up ahead.

The water was already past the windows, and I was astonished that the whole place hadn't been completely swept away. I steered myself directly at it and, as I passed, somehow managed to catch hold of a drain spout that was sticking out from the tin roof. It ripped my hand but good, and it was a hell of a struggle to hang on then hoist myself on top.

But I did it.

I don't know how long I lay there heaving up the water in my lungs and fighting to catch my breath. Finally, the convulsions of my exertion subsided, and I was able to prop myself into a sitting position.

The water wasn't rising anymore, but stretched on towards town as far as the eye could see. Without success, I tried to block out of my mind the death and destruction it was leaving in its wake.

I looked around and saw the tops of the hills, all of them, of course, much taller than the house. One lone horse stood perched atop the nearest one. It saw me, too, and both of us, soaked to the bone, engaged in a staring contest.

Several hours went by. The sun had started to sink. The mud and silt from the flood tide had settled somewhat, and so had the water level, having gone down several feet. And, when I bent over the edge of the roof, I could see the tops of the windows once more.

But as I raised my head again, something caught my eye, and it sent chills up my already shivering back.

The wagon had been rolled maybe ten yards by the force of the floodwaters and had become wedged sideways against the twin posts that supported the rickety wood porch awning. The old man was gone, nowhere in sight. The horse lay broken – drowned and strangled by its harness.

And Lucy was still there, her eyes closed, lying calm and serene in the wagon bed. One of her arms had gotten caught in the collapsed seat, and I reckon that's why she hadn't been washed away along with everything else.

For a few minutes, I felt like I was going to start bawling. Then it passed, and I realized that I just didn't have anything left inside of me. It was all used up, drained to the last drop.

I knew I wasn't going anywhere for quite a while. So I just lay there, hanging over the edge of the roof and looking at her. I watched her black hair wafting gracefully back and forth across her face and wondered at how beautiful she was – even in Death.

I watched her until the moon rose, and it became too dark. And I couldn't see her anymore.

Thank yous...

need to go out to Donna Lethal, Eve Golden, Byron Coley, Lili Dwight, Thurston Moore, Eddie Muller, Peter Maravelis, John Doe, Lydia Lunch, Grace Krilanovich, Mary Woronov, Jerry Stahl, Craig Clevenger, Alan K. Rode, Alex Maslansky, Claudia Colodro, Liz Garo, Billy Shire, Shepherd Stevenson, Benjamin Rew, Erika Wear, Dan Kusunoki, Mike Minky, Richard Modiano, Tosh Berman, Patrick Paeper at Alias Books East, Mark Rainey and Julia Smut

Chris D. is author of the novels *NO EVIL STAR, MOTHER'S WORRY, SHALLOW WATER, VOLCANO GIRLS, TIGHTROPE ON FIRE* and the collection *DRAGON WHEEL SPLENDOR AND OTHER LOVE STORIES OF VIOLENCE AND DREAD,*. His anthology *A MINUTE TO PRAY, A SECOND TO DIE*, a 500 page collection of selected short stories, excerpts from novels and scores of dream journal entries, as well as all of his poetry and song lyrics, was published in December 2009. His non-fiction *OUTLAW MASTERS OF JAPANESE FILM* was published by IB Tauris (distributed by Palgrave Macmillan in the USA) in 2005.

He saw release of his first feature film as director, *I PASS FOR HUMAN*, in 2004 (and its DVD release in 2006), and worked as a programmer at The American Cinematheque in Hollywood, California from 1999-2009.

Chris D. is also known as the singer/songwriter of the bands The Flesh Eaters, Divine Horsemen and Stone by Stone. He was an A&R rep and in-house producer at Slash Records/Ruby Records from 1980-1984.

His latest work includes the mammoth non-fiction *GUN AND SWORD: AN ENCYCLOPEDIA OF JAPANESE GANGSTER FILMS 1955-1980*

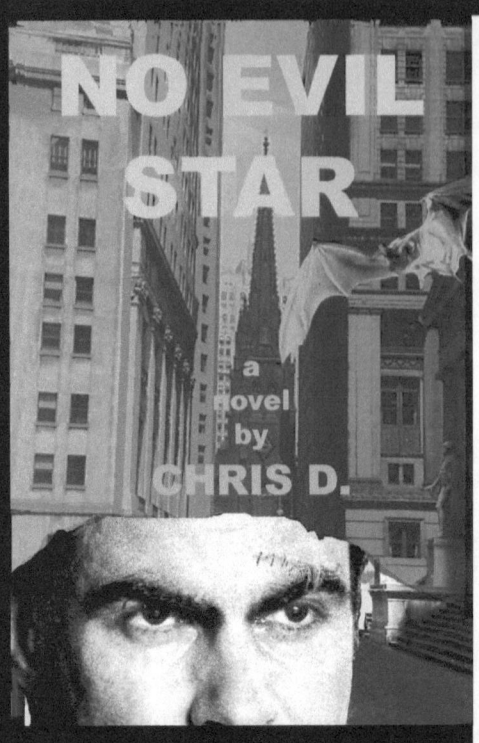

The life of recovering addict and Namvet Milo unravels when ex-CIA friend Dave goes off the deep end. Not only is Dave the heist man whacking NYC drug dealers, he's also hatching a scheme to plunder mob boss Nunzio's art treasures pilfered in WWII. Complicating matters, Yuen, an ex-Viet Cong with a grudge against Milo and Dave, arrives in New York.

"A healthy authorial sense of curiosityand generosity lends weight to No Evil Star's intersecting lives, where Chris D. ably traces out the contours of human torment in a manner recalling American films of the 1970s."
– Grace Krilanovich, author of The Orange Eats Creeps

AVAILABLE NOW FROM POISON FANG BOOKS

In Chris D.'s title novella, brilliant, alcoholic Anne, unable to succeed in downtown L.A.'s arts community, helps a Japanese-American girl escape forced prostitution, only to ignite a string of violent deaths. In "The Glider," a British policewoman falls in-love with a serial killer near the white cliffs of Dover; plus five more twisted love tales.

"...seems to shimmer with menace... with Dragon Wheel Splendor, the great Chris D should finally find the audience he deserves...a book that can kill the voices in your head - or make you love them."
– Jerry Stahl, author of Plainclothes Naked, Painkillers and Permanent Midnight

The year is 1987, and outlaw Ray Diamond's mother is the queenpin of crime in Mystic, GA. After his Navy discharge, Ray knocks over a mob-connected El Paso liquor store, not counting on Eli, the owner's psycho son, dogging his trail. Back home in Mystic, Ray's girl, Connie Eustace, resorts to stripping at Mama Lorna's club to make ends meet. Witness to a murder by the local sheriff, she goes on a drug-and-drink bender, jumping from the frying pain into the fire.

"...a crazy dive into a universe populated largely by monsters...a classic update of the Gold Medal/Lion Library loser noir tradition. Great work... "
– Byron Coley, writer for WIRE magazine, author of C'EST LA GUERRE: EARLY WRITINGS 1978-1983

MOTHER'S WORRY

a novel by CHRIS D.

FROM POISON FANG BOOKS   AVAILABLE NOW

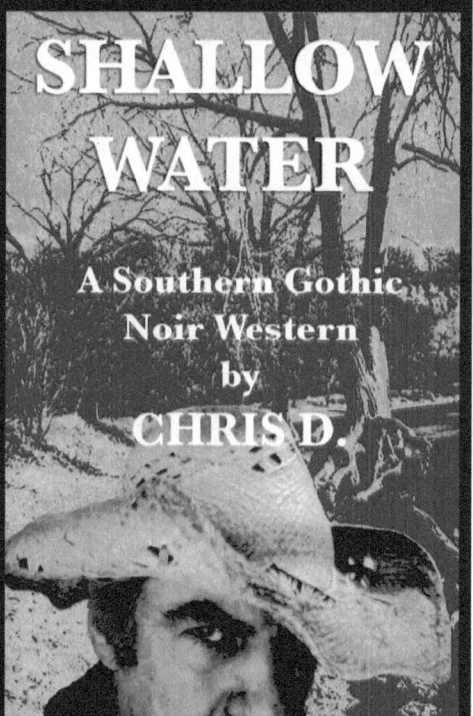

SHALLOW WATER

A Southern Gothic Noir Western by CHRIS D.

Post-Civil War, bitter rebel veteran and bounty hunter, Santo Brady, drifts through the Deep South. When he rescues halfbreed Indian prostitute, Lucy Damien, from one backwater town, he has the whole world fall in on his head. They embark on a freight-train-hopping odyssey to New Orleans, unaware that Lucy's rich white father and homicidal brother are tracking them. A tragic tall tale plunging head-first into a wild heart of darkness.

"One sinister serpent of a story, an old Republic Pictures western serial scripted by James M. Cain and reimagined by Sam Peckinpah. I loved it."
– Eddie Muller, author of THE DISTANCE and SHADOW BOXER

Two New Novels from Chris D. Available October 2013

Half-sisters, schoolteacher Mona and junkie punk rocker Terri, are uneasy roommates while taking care of their sick mother. When their boyfriends, cop Johnny Cullen and killer Merle Chambers, clash due to labor struggles in their small town of Devil's River, the two women are pulled into the fray. To make matters worse, jealous female sheriff, Billie Travers, decides Mona is intruding on her faltering love affair, and quiet small town life amps up into an apocalyptic nightmare of uncontrollable violence and destruction.

Corrupt female police detective, Frankie Powers, is treading water in her small desert hometown of Sweet Home, California. Burned-out and emotionally numb after losing her husband and child in a mysterious fire ten years before, her conscience is reawakened when her affair with a Bakersfield narc brings new facts to light. Frankie's mob boss uncle, Jack Richman, has been kidnapping under-age girls for his Vegas prostitution syndicate; he's also been victimizing his own teen daughters, Frankie's twin bad girl cousins, Valerie and Vanessa. Soon Frankie finds herself singlehand-edly fighting tooth-and-nail against not only wicked uncle Jack but also his dominatrix wife, Marilyn and their degenerate hitman, Cal Nero. Can a lone shewolf survive against the bloodthirsty pack?

from **Poison Fang Books**

www.ingramcontent.com/pod-product-compliance
Lightning Source LLC
Chambersburg PA
CBHW030508260626
47157CB00005B/1704